STARTING

EARLY

A STORY ABOUT A BOY AND HIS BUGLE
IN AMERICA DURING WWII

PAUL KIMPTON

AND

ANN KACZKOWSKI KIMPTON

GIA Publications, Inc.
Chicago

Starting Early
Paul Kimpton and Ann Kaczkowski Kimpton

Design, layout, illustrations, and cover art by Martha Chlipala

G-7850

ISBN: 978-1-57999-805-9

STARTING

EARLY

STARTING EARLY

Dale had always dreamed about playing the trumpet like Louis Armstrong. When the school didn't have enough money to fund the sixth-grade band, Grandpa stepped in. Sensing Dale's disappointment, Grandpa brought out his old cavalry bugle and taught Dale to play. Little did Dale know that these music lessons would lead to the most important performance of his life.

For our parents who instilled in us a love
of music,
the outdoors,
and adventure

For Teresa Edwards, our dear editor and friend

For Edith, our wise GIA editor

For Tommy Kaczkowski, our fun-loving nephew,
who offered suggestions

STARTING EARLY

Chapter 1

TAKE OFF

Dale could feel the cool morning air on his face as he pedaled his Schwinn Super Flyer down tree-lined Vermont Street. His dog, Scout, a black and white Border collie, galloped beside him as they flew by the large brick houses with their wraparound porches. Dale paused at the top of Simpson Hill, surveying the town of Libertyville that spread out across the valley. The dome of the courthouse, the town square with the bandstand, and all of the businesses downtown were visible from the top of this hill, which was the highest point in town.

Dale could also see the Conn musical instrument factory that was on the far side of the valley with its large smokestacks reaching to the sky. Seeing the factory reminded him that today was the day he and his friends would attend a meeting about the new school band program. Dale was excited about meeting the new band director and hearing about joining the band to learn how to play a musical instrument.

At the bottom of Simpson Hill, Dale turned right onto Main Street and looked up at the canopy of trees that lined the street leading to the firehouse. This is where he planned to meet Charlie Walsh and his dad, Joe.

Mr. Walsh was a volunteer fireman and could be found every morning at the firehouse. He always made sure that all the equipment was ready for the day and that Smokey the Dalmatian had been fed. Scout spied Charlie and Smokey first and raced ahead to meet them. Dale pedaled faster but could not keep up with Scout. The two dogs were play wrestling when Dale pulled up, slamming on the brakes and skidding to a stop.

"Nice skid," said Charlie, admiring the black tire mark on the sidewalk.

Charlie's dad yelled, "You'd better not let your mom catch you skidding your tires like that with the shortage of rubber and all."

"OK, Mr. Walsh," Dale mumbled.

Charlie moved toward Dale. "Yeah, but what a great skid mark! We'll have to show the gang after school. That reminds me—today Mr. Jeffrey, the new music teacher, is going to tell us about the new band program. I'm really excited about learning to play an instrument. But now we'd better get moving if we're going to see your mom take off before we go to school. Did you say runway 27R at 7:30?"

"Yes! Mom even wrote it down for me," Dale answered, taking out the diagram of the field and runway. "See—7:30 a.m."

Dale's mom was a pilot for the Women's Air Force Service Pilots (WASPs), which was established in August of 1943 during World War II. Charlie thought she was really neat, because she flew the newly completed B-17s and other military aircraft to Wright Field in Dayton, Ohio, where they would be tested and readied for the war in Europe and Japan. Charlie's own mom was part of the war effort too, but her work didn't seem as exciting to him. She worked at the Conn instrument plant near the airport—only now it wasn't making musical instruments. The plant had been converted to make compasses, altimeters, and gyro-horizon indicators for planes like the ones Dale's mom flew.

"Dad," Charlie asked, "can Smokey and Scout come with us to the airport before school?"

"Yes, but make sure they are tied up back at the house before you go to school."

The ride to the airport, about a mile out of town, took about 15 minutes. Scout and Smokey ran close to the boys' bikes and sniffed the cool morning air. The Air Force had built a large dirt hill around the airport to make it harder to see the planes or the guards on the tarmac where the new planes were parked. There was a huge oak tree near runway 27R, just outside the fence. The boys could climb the tree to see over the dirt hill and watch the planes land and take off. Some days the boys would sit for hours, dangling their feet from the branches, and talk about the B-17s, B-25s, and DC-3s. Today was special, however, because Dale's mom would be flying a B-17 right over their tree. Both of the dogs were lying down between the big tree roots, tired from the early morning run to the airfield. When Dale saw his mom walking to the B-17, he pointed.

"How can you tell that's your mom?" asked Charlie.

"Because she told me to look for a white scarf like Errol Flynn wears around his neck in the movies."

The boys watched her climb into the nose of the plane followed by the co-pilot, navigator, and radioman. Only four were needed to fly the plane, which usually held 10 to 13 crew members. After the crew disappeared into the plane, the boys settled back on their favorite tree limb and waited. Charlie shaded his eyes from the early morning sun as a puff of smoke came from the first of the four engines. The boys knew the order the engines would start because Dale's mom had described the pre-flight checks a crew had to perform. The first engine sputtered, and then suddenly roared to life, followed by the other three. The boys could feel the engines rumble as the B-17 taxied down the runway. When the plane reached the end of the runway, it slowly turned and faced the boys, who watched in awe from a half mile away.

"It won't be long now." Dale's voice sounded tighter than usual.

Scout was all ears as the engines began to whine and rev up. When it seemed like the sound could not get any louder, the B-17 began to move toward them down the runway. Faster and faster the plane came until suddenly it lifted into the air, rising just above the tree where the boys were perched. They could see the navigator in the glass nose of the plane. He leaned forward and gave the boys a salute. They answered by waving their arms in the air. The wind from the engines shook the tree limbs as the plane flew past them and climbed into the early morning sun.

As the sound faded, they sat in appreciation for a minute until Dale looked down and noticed that the dogs were up and waiting.

"We'd better get moving if we're going to get home to tie the dogs up and get to school on time."

Down the tree they scurried and jumped onto their bikes.

"Come on, Charlie," Dale shouted. "I'll race you to your house."

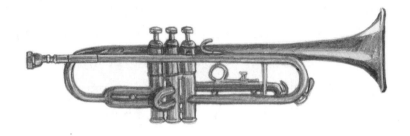

Chapter 2

SCHOOL AND THE NEW BAND MEETING

The boys pulled up to the bike rack just in time to hear the bell signaling everyone to come in from the playground. The gang—Tommy, Dave, Bobby, Victor, and Karl—all came running over to meet Dale and Charlie before going into school. They attended the Emerson School and were all in Mrs. Cooper's sixth-grade classroom. Each boy had a story about what had happened since yesterday, but none of them could beat Charlie's description of Dale's early morning skid at the fire station. They all agreed to go and have a look after the meeting with the new band director.

Dave said, "I am picking drums so I can be like Gene Krupa." Tommy wanted to play alto saxophone like Charlie Parker. Victor wanted to play French horn like Phil Farkus. Playing the clarinet like Benny Goodman was Bobby's choice. Finally, Charlie mopped his brow and shouted, "I want to play trombone like Tommy Dorsey."

All the boys looked at Dale. He held them in suspense for a minute. Then he leaned back, put his hands in the air like he was playing a trumpet and sang out, "I want to play trumpet like the great Louis Armstrong."

Everyone laughed and headed into school pretending to play the instrument they had chosen.

Mrs. Cooper greeted the boys at the door with a smile, and with a pat on the head said to Dale: "Sounds like you had some morning, watching your mom take off in a B-17. And what is this I hear about a skid mark?" Mrs. Cooper had a way of keeping up with things! Once they were all inside, she called, "Let's settle down!" And after a few remaining wiggles, they did.

School started at 8:30 a.m. with the Pledge of Allegiance, followed by math from 8:35 to 9:30. All Dale could think about was a new, shiny trumpet and all of the exciting music they would get to play. As he imagined it all, Mrs. Cooper's stern voice broke in. "Dale, can you tell us the answer to the next question in your math book?"

The words didn't register until Bridget Neilson, who had a blonde ponytail and bright blue eyes and could out-run all of the boys in the sixth grade, poked him in the back and whispered, "Dale, Mrs. Cooper is talking to you."

Dale answered, "I'm sorry Mrs. Cooper. I was thinking about the band meeting with Mr. Jeffrey today. I didn't hear your question."

Mrs. Cooper reprimanded, "Well, if I see any more daydreaming from you, you will have to stay in class to finish your work instead of going to the meeting with the rest of the students!"

"I'm sorry," Dale promised. "It won't happen again."

"I hope not! Class, let's continue. Can anyone answer the question that I asked Dale?"

Hands went up as Dale slid down in his chair, embarrassed at being caught daydreaming. At the end of math class Mrs. Cooper asked the students to open their history books to page 89 and read silently. History was Dale's favorite subject. Today, though, Dale looked at the clock expecting the end of class. Five minutes had gone by. He acted like he was reading, but his mind kept jumping to the meeting at 2:00, imagining what it would be like to play in a band. Finally, at 11:30 the bell rang for lunch, and all the students headed to the cafeteria. Tommy, Dave, Bobby, Victor, Charlie, and Karl all sat with Dale at the same lunch table.

Victor began, "Wow, Dale, did you get in trouble or what. I'm glad she didn't call on me. I was thinking about playing the French horn and not math."

Dale lamented, "I always get caught daydreaming."

"Well, better you than me!" Victor retorted. Everyone laughed.

Bobby had an idea. "After lunch, let's play some baseball. That will take our minds off of band."

"How come lunch and recess go so fast and class goes so slow?" asked Charlie as he stuffed half of a peanut butter sandwich in his mouth.

Tommy cocked his head, "Come on, Charlie. Don't talk with your mouth full. We can't understand a word you're saying."

All the boys started talking with food in their mouths like Charlie, until the principal, Mr. Prenty, marched over and urged them to mind their manners while eating. Mouths full, the boys could only nod their heads.

After lunch and a rousing game of baseball, the boys filed back into the classroom. Mrs. Cooper started with the vocabulary words for the week. She recited the words and the students wrote them down and then used them in sentences. Dale had worked hard practicing spelling and making sentences with his grandfather. He was ready to spell each word perfectly. Mrs. Cooper recited the word "elephant." As he wrote, Dale heard Mrs. Cooper's voice. "Dale, spell the word and use it in a sentence." Dale pronounced each letter precisely: "E-L-E-P-H-A-N-T," and then thought about how to use the word in a sentence.

"I've got it! The elephant leaned back and trumpeted loudly."

Karl laughed out loud, leaning back and wiggling his fingers like Dale did earlier when he was pretending to be Louis Armstrong. Mrs. Cooper quickly brought the class back under control.

"There is no question, Dale, where your mind is today."

As the afternoon wore on, Dale could swear the clock was moving backwards instead of moving closer to 2:00. Finally at 1:55 Mrs. Cooper announced, "Anyone interested in learning a musical instrument should leave class now to go to the auditorium for a meeting with Mr. Jeffrey."

Dale had waited all day for this meeting. He jumped up from his desk, knocking over his chair. Everyone turned and laughed at Dale before Mrs. Cooper could say anything.

Mrs. Cooper said knowingly, "Dale, please keep your excitement under control. I would also like to remind everyone how to act in the auditorium." Everyone knew what that meant—sit quietly and behave with respect.

After picking up his chair Dale got in line with the other students for the walk to the auditorium. Once everyone was seated, Mr. Jeffrey, a tall man with brown hair and black shiny eyes, climbed the stairs to the stage.

Bridget Nielson whispered to Dale: "My dad says that Mr. Jeffrey played in John Phillip Sousa's band *and* Edwin Franko Goldman's band before coming to Emerson School." Bridget added, "He was a great cornet soloist."

"Really? I want to play the trumpet."

Bridget whispered back, "I bet you'll be good at the cornet because that's just like a trumpet. Cornets are usually played in bands."

Dale thought for a moment. "I didn't know that. I guess I'll change from trumpet to cornet."

"I want to play the French horn."

"Hey, so does Victor," Dale replied.

When Mr. Jeffrey got to the podium a hush fell over the room, as everyone was anxious to hear the details of the new band program. Mr. Jeffrey welcomed the students and said, "I had not expected such a large turnout of interested students. With so many interested students from grades 6, 7 and 8, and a limited number of instruments, I'll have to limit the number of students who can start this first year." Suddenly the students began talking to each other about who would get to start and who would not. The talking got louder and more agitated until Mr. Jeffrey clapped his hands together. "Please, please settle down and let me explain." All the students got quiet so they could hear how they would be selected. Mr. Jeffrey said, "To be fair to everyone, I can only start 7th and 8th graders this first year."

Dale jumped up from his seat and shouted, "That's not fair!" before realizing he was the only one standing.

"I understand your disappointment but we have a limited number of instruments and money this first year," Mr. Jeffrey answered.

Bridget reached over and touched Dale's hand. "That's OK. I know it will work out for you to play the cornet."

Dale sat down dejected. He didn't hear the rest of the meeting. His thoughts were only about playing a cornet.

After the meeting as the students filed out of the auditorium, Dale felt a hand on his shoulder. He thought it was Bridget, but when he looked up, he saw Mr. Jeffrey.

"Dale," Mr. Jeffrey said. "Don't be disappointed. You'll be able to start in the summer, which is only nine months away."

Tears filled Dale's eyes. "I understand, but I really wanted to play the cornet," Dale said with a slight quiver in his voice. He quickly wiped the tears away so Mr. Jeffrey wouldn't see them. Dale headed outside where his friends were waiting by the bike rack. He felt the warm afternoon sun on his face and took a deep breath to clear his mind of his disappointment. He put his lips together and gave a huge whistle through his teeth. All the boys' heads turned. "Hey, let's go see the awesome skid mark I made this morning."

"We can swing by my house and have a peanut butter sandwich and pick up the dogs," Charlie invited. A loud "yeah" came from all the boys followed by Charlie shouting, "I'll race yah!"

The boys jumped on their bikes and tore down the street chasing Charlie, who already had a head start. Dale was in last place at the halfway point to Charlie's house but had an idea of how to win. Once everyone was far ahead, he turned and cut through the alley behind the Sinclair Gas station and then rode into the "Jungle." The Jungle was an old wooded lot with dirt hills and great places to play army and tag. It also was a shortcut to Charlie's house that no one had thought of. Dale flew down the dirt trail that ran through the center of the big wooded lot, making sure not to hit any of the logs, rocks, and limbs that were scattered all over the place.

When Dale reached the edge of the Jungle, he could hear Charlie yelling on the next street over, "I'm gonna win!"

Hearing Charlie bragging made Dale even more determined to beat him. He rode even faster now and cut through two more backyards and was in sight of Charlie's backyard and the dogs. He whistled and the dogs jumped up, pulling on their chains with excitement. He skidded to a stop, jumped off his bike, and sat down next to the dogs, pretending he had been petting the dogs for a long time.

"Hey, what took you guys so long?" Dale shouted as Charlie rode into the yard being chased by the rest of the gang.

"That's not fair to take a shortcut," Charlie yelled back.

"Yea, because you didn't think of it!" Victor retorted.

"What's all the laughter about?" Charlie's mom asked as she swung open the kitchen door.

"Hi, Mrs. Walsh. Charlie is whining again about not winning the bike race," Dave answered.

"I knew something was going on. Come in, boys. Wash up and have a snack before you go to the firehouse." Everyone ran inside, washed their hands, and dug into the hastily piled sandwiches and tall glasses of milk. When they were done, they thanked Mrs. Walsh and headed outside.

"Let's not race to the firehouse. My legs are tired," Charlie pleaded.

"Sure," Victor shouted, as everyone jumped on their bikes and took off racing to the firehouse.

Chapter 3
DUTY CALLS

Mr. Walsh was sitting outside the firehouse when the boys and the two dogs pulled up next to him. "Looks like you have been racing again by the way you're sweating," he said. "Come over here, sit down, and tell me about your school day."

The boys watched Dale carefully as he explained to Charlie's dad about not being able to start band this year because of the lack of instruments and money.

"I'm sure you're disappointed, but sometimes you don't always get what you want. Nine months really isn't that long to wait," he consoled. "What instruments do you others want to play?" Mr. Walsh listened to each boy. "Well, you sure have a lot more opportunities in school today than I had growing up. You are lucky you get to start an instrument at all."

"Hmmm, I guess you're right. It is only nine months," Victor answered.

Dale stood up. "I'd better get home. My grandfather will be waiting for me." As he took off on his bike, he shouted, "Charlie, I'll meet you here in the morning." And with a wave, he started home with Scout by his side.

Pedaling back up Simpson Hill was a lot harder than going down. As Dale neared the top of the hill, he began to think again about not getting to start an instrument. He wanted to play all the great jazz songs he heard at night on the radio with his mom and grandparents. As he rounded the corner onto Vermont Street, he could see Grandpa Rodine sitting on the big porch in his high-backed rocking chair. Most days after work on the Burlington Railroad, Grandpa Rodine would rock, reading the paper with the latest news on the war. Scout knew they were close to home and took off at breakneck speed to the house, looking forward to the possibility of the rough scratching he would get from Grandpa. Dale had enjoyed moving into Grandpa's big, old three story house since his dad had gone off to war and his mom was busy flying for the WASPs.

"Come on, come on...where's the good dog?" Grandpa Rodine called, as soon as he saw Scout flying down the sidewalk toward him. He rose out of his rocker, clapped his hands together, and yelled again, "Come on, come on...where's the good dog?"

Hearing Grandpa's voice, Scout crouched lower to the ground and moved even faster. Reaching the porch, he jumped the stairs and slid to a stop at Grandpa's feet, waiting to be scratched and petted.

"Yes, you are a good dog. You are, you really are," Grandpa cooed while scratching Scout's belly with both hands.

"Wow, that dog can move," Dale gasped as he rode up to the porch.

"He sure can," Grandpa replied. "You left early this morning. Did you get to see your mom take off?"

"Yes and she even dipped her wings for us," Dale related excitedly.

"Great," Grandpa answered. "Now come sit down, and tell me about your day."

Dale began telling Grandpa all about the ride to the firehouse, the airport, followed by how well he knew the vocabulary words they had been practicing together.

"I forgot to ask how the meeting went with Mr. Jeffrey about the new band program," Grandpa said interrupting Dale. "Are you going to get to play the cornet?"

Dale swallowed hard and tried not to show how upset he was, but he couldn't. His eyes filled with tears as he told the whole story from the beginning to end where Mr. Jeffrey patted his shoulder saying, "Don't be too disappointed. You can start this coming summer." Dale sat quietly, and his grandfather didn't say anything. The silence seemed to last forever. Maybe his grandfather didn't understand his disappointment.

"Well, I guess I'll have to teach you myself," Grandpa announced.

"You can play the cornet?" Dale asked.

"No, but I can play the bugle which is the same thing without the valves," replied Grandpa.

"But Grandpa, you never told me you played a bugle. I've never heard you play it."

"It's a long story, so I'll start from the beginning. It's easier told by showing you where I keep my Spanish-American war uniform, medals, and of course, my bugle and music," Grandpa explained as he stood up. "Let's get started." Grandpa put his arm around Dale's shoulder and said softly, "I think this will be fun for both of us."

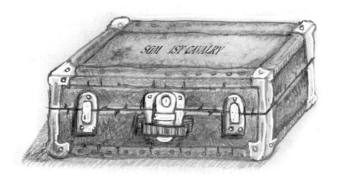

Chapter 4
THE TRUNK

Grandpa Rodine led the way up to the third floor attic, which was filled with dusty old pictures, lamps, and furniture. Several worn leather trunks were stacked in one of the corners. Dale had been in the attic a few times with his grandmother to help carry down the glass jars she used for canning vegetables and peaches each fall. On those visits to the attic, Dale didn't get a chance to explore the dark and stuffy room and his imagination was running wild about what treasure might be hidden in that trunk.

"Come on over here and help me carry this trunk down to the porch," Grandpa called as he lifted the dark green trunk with the words Sergeant Major, 1st Cavalry, painted in faded white letters on the top.

Dale had never noticed the writing before. "You were a Sergeant Major, Grandpa?"

Suddenly Grandpa's voice took on a solemn tone. "You heard me—come help."

Dale snapped to attention and responded, "Yes sir," followed by a quick salute.

Grandpa smiled, returned the salute, and commanded, "At ease, soldier. Come on, let's get going."

Sweat dripped from Dale's forehead as he helped Grandpa carry the heavy trunk down the three flights of stairs. Grandpa showed no sign of fatigue as he hoisted most of the weight. As they arrived on the porch, Grandma Alice appeared carrying a tray with two frosted glasses of lemonade and placed it on the table. She exclaimed, "You look like you worked up a sweat carrying that old trunk down from the attic!"

"Thanks, Grandma," Dale said, raising the cool glass to his lips and taking a long drink.

"You're welcome. I bet that trunk hasn't been opened in twenty years. What prompted you to bring it down now?"

"Grandpa is going to teach me how to play the bugle because Mr. Jeffrey, the new band teacher, didn't have instruments for the 6th graders. I would have to wait until summer." Dale's words brimmed over with excitement.

"Well, well," Grandma said, "your grandfather was a great bugler. Maybe it is time to have him tell you some of the great adventures he had when he was young."

Grandpa pulled up his chair and sat back, thinking. He patted the top of the trunk and said, "Let's see what we have in here." As he raised the lid the rusty hinges creaked and two leather straps kept the trunk lid from falling back.

Dale looked inside. "Wow, look at all the stuff!"

Grandpa nodded, "Yes, and each item has a story." Grandpa gently pulled out a green jacket with brass buttons down the front and a gold pin that had a hat and two swords crossing in the middle. Grandpa said, "This is my dress uniform for parades and important military functions."

The shiny pin caught Dale's eye. "What's this pin for?"

"Well, it has several meanings. First, it tells everyone that I am in the cavalry and second, it shows what division I was in." Next came out a pair of tall, shiny black boots with straps on both sides.

Grandpa explained, "These were for riding horses and helped to keep your legs from rubbing raw on the saddle." Dale was trying to put the boots on when

Grandpa pulled out a brown leather pouch that had a large pair of binoculars in it.

"These sure came in handy when I was trying to see what was going on during a battle." Dale took the binoculars out, held them to his eyes, and tried to see through the eyepieces. "Move the wheel between the lenses to adjust the focus," Grandpa advised.

Dale pointed the glasses out the window, but he could only see blurred houses and trees until he turned the center wheel. Suddenly, he could see down Simpson Hill all the way to the airfield just outside of town. "Wow, we could have used these this morning to watch Mom take off." The town looked smaller as he scanned the buildings.

Next Grandpa brought out a long black metal case containing a sword. He cautioned, "This is not a toy, so be careful because it is really sharp." As Grandpa pulled the sword out of its case, it made a metal "zing" sound like a high-pitched bell.

Dale said, "Can I hold it?"

"OK, but only with the sword in the case." Grandpa slid the sword back in the case and handed it to Dale. The sword was heavy and Dale needed to use both hands to hold it up.

"Make sure you don't swing it around. Just hold it," warned Grandpa. "You might hurt someone."

Dale admired the braided handle and the engraving on the case before handing it back.

Grandpa laid the case down gently and reached deep into the trunk, pulling out a large photo of a group of men, all in uniform. In the right corner of the picture was some white lettering that said Teddy Roosevelt and the Rough Riders.

"Where are you, Grandpa?"

Grandpa pointed to a tall, tanned man in the middle of the picture. "Here I am, right next to Teddy Roosevelt himself."

Dale had read about Teddy Roosevelt and the Rough Riders in school and said, "You really look young and tough."

"I was both," Grandpa laughed. "This was one of the most famous groups of men that ever rode together. Teddy Roosevelt even signed the photo on the back."

As Grandpa turned over the picture, Dale could see the handwriting. "What does it say?"

Grandpa read, "To C. H. with admiration. You saved our lives more than once with your bugle. Your friend forever, TR."

"Yes, Teddy and I had quite a few adventures during the Spanish American War," added Grandpa.

"Can I see the bugle now?" Dale urged impatiently.

Dale leaned over the trunk and watched Grandpa pull out a brass bugle with red braid wrapped around the top. It had two long brass tubes that made up the body, a flared opening (the bell) on one end and a mouthpiece on the other. "Hey, where are the valves?" Dale asked.

"Bugles don't have valves like a cornet or trumpet," Grandpa said, handing the bugle to Dale.

"Is this the one you actually played in the war, Grandpa?"

"Yes, and the one you will learn to play." Grandpa reached back into the trunk pulling out another bugle and said, "This bugle is the one I played at Teddy's presidential funeral in 1919." Slowly he pulled out the shiny bugle, which was engraved on the bell. The sun glinted off the bell as Grandpa said, "This one is special and is never to be played."

"That's OK, Grandpa," Dale said as he looked down at the burnished bugle in his hands. "This one is better since you used it in battle."

"Let me show you the manual. I used it to learn how to play the bugle and the many bugle calls."

Dale moved close to Grandpa and looked at the small brown leather-bound manual titled, *Cavalry Drill Regulation, United States Army.* Grandpa explained that this small book had all of the bugle calls written out in addition to all of the rules and regulations a soldier needed to learn to be in the army and cavalry.

Dale could hardly contain his excitement. "Can we open it up and look through it?"

Grandpa gently opened the manual to the page with the words *Mess Call* written on it.

Chapter 5
FIRST SOUNDS

At first, it took all of Dale's effort to make a sound on the bugle.

Grandpa advised, "Make a buzzing sound with your lips. It's kind of like when you get a bug in your mouth, and you spit it out." Dale put his lips together following Grandpa's example and out came a small "bzzz—— bzzz."

"That's close, but hold the *bzzzzzz* longer once you get it going." Dale practiced spitting and holding the buzz sound until finally he was able to hold it for a few seconds.

Grandpa then instructed, "Alright, now try and get a high buzz, then a low buzz." Dale got the high buzz but made a strange noise when he tried to make a low one.

Grandpa laughed and slapped his leg. "Well, that's close, but try to relax your lips to get the low buzz."

After several more tries, Dale could buzz high and low. "Making the buzzing sound with my lips makes them feel fuzzy and warm."

"I think that means you're ready," Grandpa said, and he handed Dale the bugle. Dale admired the worn brass finish as he gently wrapped his fingers around the lead pipe.

"Put half of the mouthpiece on your top lip and the other half on your bottom lip. Then make the buzzing sound into the mouthpiece. Be sure to hold the buzz. Don't worry about the sound that comes out of the bugle."

Dale felt nervous and sweaty as he placed the cold mouthpiece on his lips. Grandpa added, "If you need to lick your lips first, go ahead. Some people play with moist lips."

Dale ran his tongue over both lips, took a breath and made a buzzing sound on the mouthpiece, *bzzzzzz*. He was startled when a sound came out of the bell.

Grandpa said, "Keep buzzing and don't stop." Dale did as he was told and heard a sound that was high and clear. Scout let out a howl that could be heard down the block.

"Yes!" Grandpa yelled. "That was a good start."

Again and again, Dale tried playing high notes and low notes with Grandpa giving him words of encouragement.

Finally, Grandma Alice came out. "Enough of the practice. Let's have dinner, you buglers. Scout's ears need to rest for awhile."

Dale agreed, not because he was tired, but because he was starving and could smell the chicken and dumplings Grandma had made.

Grandma returned to the kitchen, pretending to play the bugle and singing, "Ta-te Ta–te Ta-Ta Ta tatata te ta,"

which was the bugle call for dinner.

Grandpa laughed and added, "Not a bad call to dinner, if I must say so. From now on Dale, you must learn your first call and that is the *Mess Call.*

"What does *mess* mean?"

"That is what the military calls dinner or where the food is served. Soldiers never want to miss out on dinner. Anyway, we will learn the *Mess Call* after dinner if Sergeant Major Grandma doesn't mind us skipping out on washing the dishes after dinner tonight."

"OK," Grandma called from the kitchen. "Let's eat. We've had enough bugle talk for now."

Chapter 6

THE RIGHT WAY

Dale realized he had a lot to learn as he read the military manual with his grandfather. As promised, Grandpa started teaching Dale by looking at the bugle call that was used to call the soldiers to dinner, the *Mess Call*.

"It's important to understand the musical symbols. If you can read and understand the symbols, you can easily read and play the music correctly." Grandpa looked directly into Dale's brown eyes. "I'm not going to teach you by rote. That's where you just hear the music and repeat it without reading the notes. All good musicians and bugle players can read music, which allows them to play songs, like the jazz we were listening to on the radio."

First, Dale had to learn the kinds of notes that made up all of the bugle calls. Dale proudly told Grandpa, "I know the note names from Mrs. Vincent's music class. The notes in the spaces of the staff spell FACE."

Grandpa encouraged, "That's right, but what about the lines of the staff?"

Dale thought for a minute. What was that phrase he had learned from Mrs. Vincent to help him remember the names of notes on the lines? Suddenly, he heard Mrs. Vincent's voice in his mind and shouted, "Every Good Boy Does Fine—EGBDF."

Grandpa laughed. "Well, you're right, but we didn't learn it that way in the Cavalry. That's a great way to remember the lines and spaces on a treble clef staff."

"What is a treble clef?" Dale asked.

Grandpa pointed at a symbol in the music. "This is a treble clef sign or G Clef. See how the symbol curls around the line where the note G is on the staff. This is the clef you will use to read music on the bugle."

Grandpa gestured to some notes on the page. "Can you tell me what these are?"

"Sure," answered Dale. "Those are quarter notes. They are solid black and have a stem. The symbol next to the quarter notes that looks like a lighting bolt is a quarter rest."

"Good, but how about the notes in the first measure or bar of the *Mess Call*?"

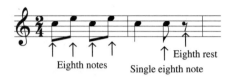

Eighth notes   Single eighth note   Eighth rest

Dale answered, "Those are eighth notes because they are solid black with a stem and are played twice as fast as quarter notes. Two eighth notes next to each other have a beam joining them. If there is only one note, it has a little flag on the end. The symbol next to the notes that looks like a seven is an eighth rest."

Dale pointed at the third bar of the music and said, "What are those notes? I don't think Mrs. Vincent taught us that."

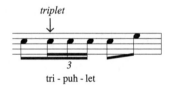

triplet

3

tri - puh - let

"Those are sixteenth-note triplets or tuplets," Grandpa explained adding, "they sound like the word triplet. Say each part of the word like this, 'tri–puh–let.'"

Dale repeated the word several times until he could run the word together and get the sounds correct. "I like triplets—they're fun to say."

Grandpa added, "We have a few more symbols to learn, and then that will be enough for one day. Look at the beginning of the music. What does the number combination $\frac{2}{4}$ mean?"

"I've never seen that before. I've only seen a $\frac{4}{4}$ symbol in Mrs. Vincent's class," Dale responded cautiously.

"Well, what did the top 4 mean in $\frac{4}{4}$?" Grandpa asked encouragingly.

"The top number is the number of beats in a measure and the bottom 4 is the type of note that gets one beat. A 4 on the bottom means a quarter note gets one beat."

"Very good, so can you guess what $\frac{2}{4}$ means?"

Dale thought for a minute and replied, "Hmmm...if the bottom number is a 4 just like $\frac{4}{4}$, it must mean that a quarter note still gets one beat."

"Correct...but what about the 2 on top?"

After a pause, Dale decided, "I'm going to guess that maybe there are only two beats in a measure. I see that the bar line is placed every other beat." Dale pointed to the bar lines on the page.

Bar line   Bar line

"Absolutely right," said Grandpa. "That school is really doing a great job of teaching you music. Now that we have learned all the musical symbols in the *Mess Call*, let's do one last thing before bedtime. I want to teach you how to count the music so you can practice learning how the music sounds."

Grandpa continued, "Eighth notes are counted *1-and-2-and*, followed by quarter notes counted *1–2–*, and the triplet bar counted *1–tri-pl-et–2-and*. You can write out the counting pattern under the notes. When you do, write them like this: *1+ 2+* with a "+" sign standing for "and." Now let's count it out together to hear how the *Mess Call* sounds."

Dale wrote the counting pattern under the notes. Then he and Grandpa read them out loud together.

"Bully for you," said Grandpa. "Now repeat the same rhythm three times in a row. Notice that the last four bars are the same except that the last note has a symbol above the staff that looks like a bird's eye peeking over it. That's called a *fermata* and it tells you to hold the note out about twice as long. Now say the note names."

Dale haltingly said, "C-E-C-E-C-C-rest-C-C-C-C-C-E-C-rest."

"OK, enough for one day," Grandpa finally said. "Tomorrow I want you to practice counting out the rhythms and the note names."

Dale's head was spinning from all the notes and counting.

Grandpa advised, "Practice buzzing your lips during the day. We'll practice playing the bugle when I get home from the railroad."

"OK," Dale promised as he started up the stairs. Stopping halfway up, Dale turned and added, "Thanks, Grandpa. This turned into a great day."

Grandpa smiled and said softly, "I enjoyed it, too. Now off to bed you go."

Today's Lessons:
Math
Reading
Vocabulary
History

Chapter 7

PRACTICE THE BASICS

When Dale got up the next morning, he ran downstairs to tell his grandfather about his dream of playing the bugle. But when he got down to the breakfast table, Grandma told him that Grandpa had already left for the railroad.

Dale was disappointed but sat down to a hearty breakfast of oatmeal and fresh-squeezed orange juice. He took out the sheet of counts and notes that he had made the night before with Grandpa Rodine. As he ate his oatmeal, he kept saying the counts and note names in his head until he could recite the *Mess Call* without stumbling. He asked Grandma, "Can I say the counts for you before I go to school?"

"Sure," Grandma replied, wiping her hands on her apron and pulling up a chair next to him.

"OK, here goes!" Dale began reading the counts he had written on his staff paper.

1 + 2 + 1   2 + 1 tri pl et 2 + 1   2

Grandma was impressed. "That's really good for only one day, but make sure you say the note names like I heard Grandpa tell you."

Saying the names of the notes was harder since Grandpa had told him not to write them under the notes. He wanted Dale to say them from memory. Dale started slowly saying each note name.

C E C E   C C rest   C C C C C E   C   rest.

"Keep practicing, honey. Grandpa will be proud of you when he hears how well you're doing. Now off you go to school and remember to come home when you hear the Conn factory whistle blow at 5:00. Your mom will be back from flying the bombers to Dayton. She'll want to see you and hear all about the things that have happened since she left yesterday."

Dale was out the door and on his bike with Scout running by his side before Grandma could finish talking. He yelled across the yard, "I'll be on time." As he rode down Simpson Hill to pick up Charlie, his head was full of notes and counts from the *Mess Call*. No one was on the street, so he practiced buzzing his lips both high and low. About half way to the firehouse, Dale thought that he might try buzzing a song or two he knew. The first song he tried was *Mary Had a Little Lamb*. Dale buzzed the first part of the song but had a hard time getting up to the high notes. As he practiced buzzing the song again, he did not hear Charlie riding up behind him on his bike.

Just as he was getting to the difficult part, Charlie yelled, "Hey, Dale, what's all that noise you're making with your lips?"

Startled, Dale slammed on his brakes, skidding to a stop. "You scared me half to death, Charlie."

"Sorry, Dale, but you were making these really strange sounds with your lips and you didn't hear me coming. What was that noise?"

Dale told him how his Grandpa was teaching him to play the bugle. He gave Charlie a quick demonstration of how to buzz his lips. Charlie asked, "Do you think you can teach me how to do that?"

"OK, but first let me learn how myself, and then I'll show you. Come on. Let's hurry up to the firehouse and drop off Scout with Smokey before school."

As the boys pulled up to the firehouse, Charlie's dad and Smokey, the firehouse Dalmatian, were just arriving along with Slim and Bud, the other volunteer firemen. Smokey ran to meet Scout, sniffed him, and play-bit his ear. That was the signal that Smokey wanted to play, and the dogs started chasing one another as Dale yelled, "Hi Mr. Walsh."

Joe Walsh turned to answer, but Charlie cut him off by saying, "Dad, Dale's learning to play the bugle."

Dale said quickly, "Come on, Charlie. You don't have to tell everyone."

"You're learning to play the bugle? I thought Mr. Jeffrey was not going to let the 6th graders start an instrument this fall."

"I'm not learning the bugle at school," Dale said proudly. "My grandfather was a bugle player for Teddy Roosevelt and the Rough Riders. He is teaching me."

Mr. Walsh was impressed. "That sounds like fun." Then he added, "Don't bugle players have calls for just about everything?"

"Yes, but right now I'm only learning the *Mess Call*, which signals dinner is ready."

"That's a good idea—start with one and then add other calls as you go," Charlie's dad said thoughtfully. "Do you think they have a call for fire?"

"I don't know, but my grandpa has a cavalry drill regulation book with all the calls. I'll see if I can find out."

"Well, if there is one, you'll have to learn it and show all the other volunteer firemen what it sounds like."

"As soon I learn my first call, I'll come and play it at the firehouse," Dale promised.

Joe Walsh turned to Charlie and tousled his hair, "Hurry up, boys, and tie the dogs up behind the station. You don't want to be late for school."

The boys corralled the dogs and fastened them on a rope. Then, jumping on their bikes, they raced the four blocks to school. As they pulled up to the bike rack, Tommy, Dave, Bobby, Victor, and Karl were waiting for them. As always, they were eager to catch up with one another since their last meeting at the fire station the day before.

Before Dale could even get off his bike, Charlie blurted out, "Guess what. Dale is learning the bugle from his grandpa." The boys all crowded around Dale and Charlie to hear more.

Dale sighed, "Come on Charlie. That is twice you told everyone I was learning to play." He looked Charlie in the eye. "Can you promise not to tell anyone else until I have learned to play a song? Let's keep it a secret between the firehouse volunteers and the gang."

"OK, cross my heart and hope to die, stick a needle in my eye," promised Charlie.

Then all the boys recited together, "Cross my heart and hope to die, stick a needle in my eye."

"Wow, your grandpa can really play the bugle?" Victor's voice had a tone of awe.

Dale explained how he was learning the *Mess Call* for dinner first.

All the boys agreed that Dale was really lucky to be able to start an instrument early. Always planning ahead, Bobby asked, "Will you be able to play the bugle like they do in the cowboy movies we see every Saturday at the Orpheum?"

Dale nodded. "Hooray!" Bobby said. "That bugle will make playing army in the Jungle a lot more fun."

The bell rang and Mrs. Cooper called across the schoolyard, "Come in, children. Please settle down. Everyone seems rather loud today." The teacher patted the head of each child who passed through the entrance to the school. Knowingly she asked, "Is there anything you want to tell me?"

Dale gave Charlie a wink, and they both said, "No. We're just excited from the bike ride this morning."

As the students moved to their desks, Bobby whispered to Dale, "I wish I had a grandpa that played the bugle. Could you teach all of the gang how to play?"

Dale thought for a moment, "OK, but give me some time to get good at it first."

Inside the classroom, everyone got busy with schoolwork. The day's lessons included math, reading, vocabulary, and, Dale's favorite, history. During each lesson, if he finished his work early, Dale would get out some paper and draw a staff. Then he would practice writing out the counts and notes of the *Mess Call*. He wanted to be ready to show his grandpa what he had learned. His pencil was getting dull and needed sharpening, so he got up to go to the pencil sharpener in the front of the room. Bridget was already sharpening her pencil when he arrived.

"Hey, Bridget. How are you?" Dale whispered.

Bridget responded, "I'm fine, but I hear you are learning to play the bugle."

"Did Charlie tell you that?"

Bridget replied, "Yes, but he made me promise to cross my heart and hope to die, stick a needle in my eye not to tell anyone else." She glanced down shyly at her shoes. "I'm looking forward to hearing you play someday."

Dale blushed. "Well, as soon as I get good enough, I'll ride over and play the first song I'm learning. It's called the *Mess Call*."

"Great," she said as she turned to go back to her seat. "I'll look forward to hearing it."

Dale finished sharpening his pencil and started back to his desk only to find Mrs. Cooper standing there with her arms crossed.

As he got closer, Mrs. Cooper took off her glasses, a sign that he was in big trouble.

Dale swallowed hard and stammered, "I... I... I... had to sharpen my pencil. I'm sorry, Mrs. Cooper, that I didn't ask your permission first."

Mrs. Cooper did not answer right away, which made Dale start to sweat. Finally, Mrs. Cooper pulled a sheet of paper from behind her back and tapped it with her glasses, demanding, "What is this, young man?"

Dale felt a little clutch in his stomach. She had found the music notes he had been working on during class. He explained, "I had finished my work, and so I was practicing writing out the notes and counts to the *Mess Call* I'm learning on the bugle with my grandfather." Again Mrs. Cooper did not answer right away, so Dale quickly added, "I'm really sorry to have been working on it during study time, but I'm so excited that I just had to practice writing out all the great things I'm learning."

Mrs. Cooper leaned down and whispered in his ear so the other students could not hear what she said. "Well, I suggest you keep your attention on your schoolwork and nothing else, or we'll have to have a talk with Principal Prenty about this kind of behavior."

"I'm really sorry, Mrs. Cooper. It won't happen again."

"For the time being, I'll keep this paper. You can come up at the end of the day and get it. Now please get back to your work."

Mrs. Cooper continued to walk down the aisles, stopping at Charlie's desk where she got after him for listening in on what she had been discussing with Dale. Dale wiped the sweat away from his forehead and picked up his pencil, but he still could not keep his mind off the notes Mrs. Cooper had taken away from him. The second hand on the clock barely moved each time he looked up. His mind kept thinking about playing the bugle when he got home. When the school bell finally rang at 3:30, all the boys and girls ran out to their bikes while Dale stayed behind and waited to talk to Mrs. Cooper.

While she erased the chalkboard, she gently asked Dale, who was normally a very good student, what had happened.

Dale slid his chair back from his desk. The legs on the wooden floor made a large scraping sound in the empty room. He walked up to her large desk and stood in front of her waiting, expecting her voice to get stern and for her to scold him.

Finally she said, "You know that working on your music notes and counts in class was wrong don't you?"

"Yes I do, but I was just so excited I didn't think about it being wrong."

"I understand," Mrs. Cooper said. "I was the same way when I started learning the flute many years ago."

Dale was surprised. "You can play the flute, Mrs. Cooper?"

"Yes, I almost majored in music at the University of Illinois before deciding to go into teaching."

"Could you play your flute for the class sometime?"

"We'll see, but let's keep the focus on you for now. I want you to promise that you will not work on your music in class." She handed Dale the crinkled notebook paper. "Here…use this at home. I also want you to promise that when you are good enough, you will come and play for the class. Maybe I'll join you and bring my flute."

Dale said eagerly, "I'll work really hard for you, Mrs. Cooper."

"OK, now get going. All of your friends are looking in the window at us. I think they want to get going to the Jungle and work on the fort," Mrs. Cooper said.

Dale took the notes, slid them into his math book and turned to go. He stopped and asked her, "How did you know they wanted to work on the fort?"

Mrs. Cooper smiled. "Nothing goes on in class that I don't hear or see."

Dale ran to meet Victor, Bobby, Charlie, Karl, and Tommy at the bike rack. They headed to the firehouse to pick up the dogs. All the boys wanted to hear what Mrs. Copper had said, but Dale brushed them off. "It was just some music stuff."

As they neared the fire station, the dogs were up and ready for a good run to the Jungle. Charlie untied Scout and Smokey. Charlie's dad had saved some old tools and scrap lumber in a box at the rear of the firehouse for the boys to use. They picked out the wood and tools they wanted to use to build their fort and each boy grabbed his share. Dragging the lumber or holding a bundle of tools with one hand and steering the bikes with the other, they rode the six blocks to the Jungle.

Everyone was exhausted from the ride when they arrived, and they dropped their bikes and gear and flopped onto the ground, panting. But Dale commanded, "Let's put the sides on the fort before it gets too late."

Victor, Bobby, and Charlie began sawing lumber while Tommy, Karl, and Dale hammered the sides into place. After an hour of hard work, they all stepped back to admire the newly finished fort.

Victor said, "This is the best fort yet. We should plan a big game of Capture the Flag for Saturday."

Dale was about to say something when they heard the shriek of the Conn factory whistle. He began quickly picking up the tools. "I have to get home. Can you guys take the tools back to the firehouse so I can get home in time for dinner?"

Charlie corrected him. "Don't you mean 'mess'?"

Dale pretended to play the bugle and sang the *Mess Call*, "Tah te tah te tah tah, tah tahtahtah te tah." Everybody laughed as he jumped on his bike with Scout at his heels. As he got to the top of Simpson Hill, Dale could see his grandpa and his mom on the porch talking and reading the paper. Scout took off at a dead run to the porch, wanting to get his daily scratching from Grandpa.

Scout was at Grandpa's feet getting scratched as Dale jumped off his bike and into his mom's arms. She had been gone for only two days, but it seemed like forever. "I hear you have some exciting things to tell me," Mom said as she gave Dale a big hug.

Dale began telling her all about the last two days, starting with how he and Charlie watched her take off in the new B-17 Bomber. Dale talked all the way through dinner and when he was done his mom said, "After all that excitement, I guess I will let you and Grandpa skip washing the dinner dishes, so you two can get busy with your next bugle lesson."

Grandpa winked at Dale. "I didn't think teaching you how to play the bugle would get us out of doing the dishes, but that's how it's working out." Dale took Grandpa's hand and led him away from the table to the living room to start the lesson.

Chapter 8

GETTING INTO THE PRACTICE MODE

Grandpa sat down in his dark leather easy chair next to the fireplace and paged through the *Bugle and Cavalry Drill Regulations* manual. Dale ran upstairs and got the crumpled staff paper he had written his counts and music on. He didn't mention that he'd been reprimanded for working on it during school. . . .

"Let's hear you buzz your lips," Grandpa began.

Dale licked his lips, took a deep breath, put his lips together and produced a buzz that must have lasted 15 seconds.

"Great, now buzz a low note for me."

Dale pursed his lips, but this time it was harder to hold it out as long.

"Don't worry about how long you can hold the buzz," Grandpa said. "Just concentrate on making the buzz clear and the air steady."

Dale tried the low buzz again, concentrating on the sound and keeping the air steady. It worked, and the sound was much better.

"Before we try buzzing the mouthpiece, we should practice a low buzz to a high buzz and back down again. Don't stop between the high and low buzz." Grandpa demonstrated buzzing from high to low. He did it several times and then said, "OK, Dale, your turn."

Dale was able to do the low buzz up to the high buzz, but had trouble coming back down.

"Keep trying, son. Don't give up. This is how you will build up the lip muscle you'll need to play the bugle."

Dale practiced again and again until he could go up and down twice before running out of air. Grandpa patted his back. "What you just did is called a lip slur. It's an exercise you should do every day with your lips and with the mouthpiece."

Grandpa drew a staff with two notes, a G and a C. "A lip slur looks like this. The curved line in between the two notes is a slur symbol. It tells a musician to keep a continuous sound between the two notes."

Grandpa handed Dale the mouthpiece. "Do you remember what I taught you last night?"

Dale placed the mouthpiece in the center of his lips, with half of the mouthpiece on the upper lip and the other half on the bottom lip.

"That's right. Now make the buzz sound on the mouthpiece," Grandpa encouraged. Dale did as he was told and out came a really high clear sound. "Good, now remember we also want low notes on the mouthpiece."

Dale relaxed his lips and buzzed low like he had without the mouthpiece. A low clear sound came out. Dale looked up at Grandpa expectantly. "OK, now do the lip slur, going back and forth and holding each note for two counts. Be sure to keep the air steady." Grandpa quickly drew six half notes on the staff with a whole note at the end. "Remember, half notes get two beats and whole notes get four beats."

It took Dale several tries, but finally he could go back and forth four to five times before running out of air. He looked at Grandpa. "My lips are really warm and tingly. They feel strange."

"That feeling is normal," Grandpa admitted. "But let's rest your lips and review the notes and counts you were going to work on."

Dale recited the counts as his fingers followed the music on the staff paper. When he finished the two lines of music, he looked up and smiled. "What do you think of that?"

Grandpa patted Dale's head. "I think you're going to be great if you keep up the hard work. Now for the hard part—I want you to say the note names this time. Don't worry about how fast you go, but do make sure you say them steady and at the same speed."

Dale recited the note names slowly and could get all the way through without forgetting any of them.

Grandpa handed Dale the bugle. "Now carefully put the mouthpiece in the bugle, making sure you don't jam it into the lead pipe. Just put it in lightly and give it a tiny twist to set it in." Dale did as he was instructed. "Let's see what your buzz sounds like when you buzz into the mouthpiece in the bugle."

Dale licked his lips and buzzed into the bugle. A sound came out that surprised both Dale and Grandpa. Dale stopped playing, and neither one said anything for a second.

Dale's mom came into the room, wiping her hands on a dishtowel. "Wow, Dad, you sound great."

Grandpa smiled. "That wasn't me Ruth—that was Dale."

Dale quickly put the bugle to his lips and played another long clear note.

Her look expressed both surprise and pride. "Well, I have to say you sure are talented. You also have a great teacher to get you to sound so good so fast."

Grandpa laughed. "Enough with the compliments— let's get back to work." As the lesson went on, Grandpa had Dale practice the lip slurs on the bugle the way he had on the mouthpiece. Finally, Grandpa announced, "Now we are going to make sure that you can hear the difference between the three notes you need to play in the *Mess Call*." Grandpa drew another staff and several notes on the page.

"The low note is G, which is the low sound you have been making tonight. Can you make the sound of a G?" Dale played the low note.

"Remember what it sounds like so you can repeat it when I'm not here. The next note up is C, which is the one you have been slurring up to." Dale tried the C but got the G again instead. Before Grandpa could say anything, Dale remembered to tighten his lips in order to get the higher sound. He did it again and this time the C came out. "Now play G then C," Grandpa instructed. After several tries, Dale finally had the hang of it.

The lesson continued with Grandpa and Dale working until it was time for bed. "Tomorrow night we will work on these notes again and then learn how to tongue each note."

Curious, Dale asked, "What does that mean, 'tongue each note'?"

Grandpa replied mysteriously, "I guess you'll find that out tomorrow."

"I can't wait," Dale said, as he gave Grandpa a hug. "I have another question. Charlie's dad asked me if there was a bugle call for a fire, but I said I didn't know."

Grandpa opened the manual and pointed to the page that said Alarms. "There are three alarm calls: "Fire,"

"To Arms," and "To Horse." If you take a look at the rest of the book, you will see all kinds of calls for different things. You can learn the *Fire Call* next after the *Mess Call*."

"Super," Dale said, "I can tell Mr. Walsh the good news on the way to school tomorrow."

Grandma and Mom walked into the living room. Grandma's eyes were twinkling. "How about you play the call for bedtime? Do you know that one?"

Grandpa picked up the bugle and played a song.

"Hey," Dale said. "I know that song. It's called *Taps*. It's the call that is played at funerals."

"You're half right," Grandpa acknowledged. "Originally it signaled lights out or the day is done. It was not until after the Civil War that it became associated with funerals. The words are written here in the manual, although I have heard other verses used."

Dale sat on the arm of the chair. Grandpa cleared his throat before he read the words, remembering how he played *Taps* for President Teddy Roosevelt's funeral in 1919.

Dale listened as Grandpa began to softly sing the words.

"I never realized that *Taps* had words that went with the music," Dale said as he put his arm around Grandpa's shoulders. "It's kind of a sad song, don't you think?"

"Well, I don't think it's sad. The words should remind us that each day is special and that we shouldn't take our lives for granted." Grandpa flipped through the pages of the manual. "Most of the bugle calls have words that go with the music."

"Even the *Mess Call* has words?"

"Yes, and they're rather funny." Grandpa opened to the page with the *Mess Call* and sang the words.

Dale laughed. "That really is silly. Can we read some more?"

Grandpa looked over at Ruth who was pointing to the clock. "Let's not do it tonight."

Dale gave his mother and Grandpa a hug and ran upstairs singing "Soupy, soupy, soupy without a single bean." As he climbed into bed, he thought about the *Fire Call*, the note names, and the counts. Finally, he laid his head down on his pillow, forgetting that he was still in his school clothes. He thought about what Grandpa had said about making each day special and enjoying every minute. Today had been special indeed—and he fell fast asleep.

Chapter 9

THE WORD SPREADS

When Dale came downstairs for breakfast Grandma was singing "Soupy, Soupy, Soupy..."

Dale laughed. "The words to the *Mess Call* really are funny Grandma."

She agreed and set a steaming bowl of hot oatmeal with brown sugar in front of him. "Do you want some milk on it?" Grandma asked.

"Sure...that will help cool it off. It's really hot." He looked up as he blew on the cereal. "Where is Mom?"

"Your mom left early because the pilots are practicing touch-and-go routines this morning at the Air Force base with some of the new B-17 pilots. She wanted to get started early while the air was still cool and the wind was calm."

Dale asked, "What are touch-and-go routines Grandma?"

"Touch and goes are when a pilot practices landing and taking off." She gestured with a flat hand swooping downward to the table like a plane landing and then back up off the table. "See, you touch down or land and go right back up or take off again. Touch and go."

Dale said, "I think Charlie and I have seen the pilots practicing those from the big oak tree at the Air Force base."

"I'm sure you have," she said. "The pilots do it quite often."

"What about Grandpa, did he already go to work on the railroad?"

"Yes, he and Mr. Paulson, the fireman on the freight train, are taking the train to Marblehead today to load it full of soy beans."

Dale said wistfully, "I hope someday Grandpa will give me a ride on the big switch engine he drives."

"Maybe someday, Dale," Grandma answered as she sipped her coffee.

Dale finished his breakfast and stepped outside, letting out a long high whistle through his teeth. He had hardly finished the whistle when Scout came flying around the house and jumped up into his arms licking his face. "Come on, Scout! I've got my school clothes on." Dale set Scout back on the ground and got on his bike and started to head to the firehouse. When Dale turned to go down Simpson Hill, Chrissy Rule, one of the girls in his class, was coming out of her house.

Chrissy was about four or five inches taller than most of the boys in Dale's class and had long brown hair that was blowing in the wind. "Hey, Dale," Chrissy yelled, and Dale skidded to a stop next to the curb.

Chrissy leaned down to greet Scout saying, "I heard you whistle and knew you would be coming down the street."

"Really, I didn't think it was that loud," Dale said.

"Yes it is. I can hear your whistle in the house when you whistle for Scout," Chrissy added.

Scout liked Chrissy because she always gave him a big scratch on his belly and rubbed him behind his ears.

"You are one spoiled dog with all the attention people give you." Scout rolled over as she reached down to scratch him. As Chrissy scratched Scout she said, "I heard you playing the bugle last night."

Dale looked surprised. "I told Bridget and Charlie not to tell anyone."

"They didn't tell me," Chrissy explained. "My parents and I heard all this sound coming from your house last night. We walked over and could see you and your grandpa playing the bugle in the living room. It sure is loud, even louder than your whistle."

"Sorry," Dale said looking down at his feet.

"Oh no, don't be sorry. It sounded really good. Next year I want to play the flute or baritone if Mr. Jeffrey lets me."

"I like both of those instruments," Dale said earnestly. "I'd better get going if I am going to meet Charlie at the firehouse before school."

"Not so fast, Dale. Remember that today after school you wanted to try and beat me in the 50-yard dash."

Dale said, "I didn't forget. I'm ready for you this time."

Both Chrissy and Bridget had beaten Dale and the other boys the last five times they had raced. The group had decided that every Friday after school, the boys and girls would all go to the track by the school and race. Since he ran the slowest, Charlie chose to be the starter. He was great at saying, "On your mark—Get set—Go!" Dale was tired of losing and watching Chrissy's long brown hair fly by him as she passed him to win every time.

"I'll be there after school, and this time I'll win," Dale exclaimed.

Chrissy flipped her hair away from her sparkling brown eyes and smiled.

"Isn't that what you said the last five times we've raced?"

They both laughed as Dale jumped back on his bike, "See you at school."

Chrissy turned to give Scout one last scratch, but Scout was up and running after Dale as he rode down Simpson Hill to the firehouse.

Charlie was sitting on the curb with Smokey by his side as Dale rode up, slamming on his brakes and skidding to a stop right next to Charlie's legs.

"Hey, you almost hit me," Charlie said as he got up from the curb.

"Almost only counts in horseshoes and hand grenades," Dale said. They both laughed and went inside the firehouse to tell Mr. Walsh they were leaving for school.

Mr. Walsh was rolling up the hoses as the boys approached. "Dale, I could hear you practicing last night from my house."

"Really?" Dale was surprised because his house was at least eight blocks away from Charlie's.

Mr. Walsh replied, "Well, maybe the wind was just right, but we could hear you. It sounded good."

"Thanks," said Dale. "I asked my grandpa about the *Fire Call* and he said there is one. I'll learn it next. He even said it has words to go with it."

"The other volunteers will be anxious to hear you when you're ready," Mr. Walsh added. "Now finish tying up Scout and Smokey before you go to school. You don't want to be late. Remember, the saying..."

Both boys recited in unison, "To be on time is to be late and to be early is to be on time."

"Good job—now off you go." Mr. Walsh waved as the boys rode toward school.

On the way, Dale taught Charlie the funny words for the *Mess Call*. By the time they got to school, Charlie could sing all the words with Dale. They stopped singing before getting to the bike rack, since they both agreed the gang would not understand how they could be singing such a silly song this early in the morning.

Victor rode up behind them as they neared the school and said, "Come on, let's race."

Dave saw them coming and yelled, "Come on, Victor. You can beat them." All the boys were yelling when Victor beat Charlie and Dale by about two feet. The boys slammed on their brakes, skidded to a stop at the bike rack, and then tried to catch their breath.

Just then, Bridget walked by and said over her shoulder, "You'd better rest up for the big race. You boys look mighty tired."

The boys all laughed and locked up their bikes for the day. Once inside Mrs. Cooper's room, everyone got into their reading groups. Dale liked the book, but he never liked to read out loud as it made him sweat. First to read was Victor, followed by Chrissy, and then Charlie. By the time it was Dale's turn, his forehead was covered with drops of perspiration. He had practiced reading out loud with his mom but he was still nervous. Dale started out slowly, but after a few sentences and no mistakes, he relaxed and got all the way through the paragraph without Mrs. Cooper interrupting to correct him.

Mrs. Cooper said, "Nice job, Dale. It looks like you have been practicing your reading, and from what I heard on my front porch last night, you were also practicing the bugle."

Dale was surprised. "Does everybody hear me playing at night?"

Victor added, "I heard you, too, and it sounded good."

"Thanks," Dale answered, "but let's keep it a secret."

Mrs. Cooper shook her head. "I think your secret is out of the bag, if I do say so myself."

The students laughed and moved back to their individual seats for spelling and math lessons.

As she sat down in the seat next to Dale, Bridget leaned over and whispered, "I heard you playing last night also, and you do sound great."

"Thanks," Dale blushed. "I'll be sure to come over after I learn my first call and play it for you." He looked down at the spelling paper, concentrating on the words in front of him, afraid to look Bridget in the eyes.

Chapter 10
THE BIG RACE

The rest of the day went quickly. Everyone was excited about the race after school and going to the movies on Saturday morning. As the time got closer to 3:30, the chatter in the classroom increased.

Finally, Mrs. Cooper raised her voice and said loudly, "Now students, we still have 15 minutes of learning left, so let's quiet down." Mrs. Cooper rarely raised her voice, but sometimes it was the only way to get the class back on task. The students got quiet and tried to finish the writing assignment they had been given for homework.

At the sound of the bell, Dale, Charlie, Tommy, Karl, Dave, Bobby, Victor, Chrissy, and Bridget all headed out to the track for the big race. They were all laughing on the way, but once they arrived, they all got quiet and serious.

The boys were looking for a win over the girls, who had won the last five times.

"OK," Charlie said, acting like their gym teacher Mr. Cabutti, "let's line up in our lanes."

Dale moved to line up between Chrissy and Bridget so he could keep an eye on them to make sure he stayed ahead. Slowly the racers lined up and got down in the starting position they had learned from Mr. Cabutti.

Charlie wiped his forehead, mimicking Mr. Cabutti, and barked, "On your mark—Get set—Go!!"

Dale slipped on the cinder track with his first step and watched in dismay as the girls surged ahead. Quickly he regained his footing and began running, realizing he was in last place by that one step. He lowered his head and began moving ahead. First he caught Victor, then Tommy; but it took a few more feet before he caught up to Bobby and Karl. Dave, Chrissy, and Bridget were just barely ahead at the halfway point. Dale had to pick them off one at a time, and Dave was next. He inched by Dave and began closing in on Chrissy and Bridget. The two girls were still one step ahead with fifteen yards to go. If only Dale could keep up his pace, he might be able to run them down. Gradually, he began to make up one inch at a time, until he was even with the girls' hair, which was flying behind them as they ran for the finish line. Dale had only a few feet left to catch them when he felt a huge wind come from behind that seemed to push him forward even faster. As he concentrated on the finish line, he could not see Chrissy and Bridget, but he could hear their feet on the cinders. They were very close.

Tony, a 7th grader, was at the finish line to decide the winner of the contest. As the three crossed the line, Tony yelled, "It's a tie, it's a tie!"

Dale, Chrissy and Bridget all slowed down and tried to catch their breath while the rest of the runners crossed the finish line.

Victor was jumping up and down yelling, "I finished fourth, I finished fourth!" For Victor, that was like winning the entire race. The other boys just put their hands on their hips and gasped for air.

Chrissy, Bridget, and Dale, their chests still heaving, walked up to Tony and said, "Did you say we tied?"

"Yup, believe it or not, you were all tied as you crossed the finish line. I could not see any clear winner."

Dale reached his hand out and shook Chrissy's and then Bridget's hand saying, "Good race...at least I didn't lose."

The two girls answered, "Well, at least we didn't lose either, so I guess we'll meet again next Friday?"

Everyone agreed to meet the following Friday for another race. As they walked back to the bike rack, they agreed that this was the best race so far, and laughed about Charlie acting and talking like Mr. Cabutti. All the boys headed off in different directions, since tomorrow they'd see each other at the movies and then at their new fort in the Jungle. Chrissy and Bridget walked off toward the Libertyville Public Library.

Charlie and Dale rode to the fire station to pick up Scout and Smokey. When they got to the firehouse, Mr. Walsh was busy working on the generator that powered the siren if the electricity went out for any reason. The siren was on a high pole on the side of the fire station and when there was a fire, the siren would be used to call all the volunteer firefighters to come get the equipment. When it went off, people could hear it all across town, even inside the houses.

Charlie asked, "What's wrong with the generator, Dad?"

"I'm not sure but I think I fixed the problem for now."

Scout and Smokey started wagging their tails and panting as soon as they saw Charlie and Dale. After being untied, they chased and play bit one another. Dale said to

Charlie, "I'd better get home. We'll be at the movies and playing at the fort most of tomorrow."

"Great!" Charlie answered. "Meet me here at 10:00 a.m. sharp, and we can meet the gang at the movies. Be sure to tie Scout up at your house before you come. I don't want the dogs here at the firehouse until we get done. We'll just get both of them after the movie and bring them to the Jungle."

Dale hopped on his bike. His legs were really tired after the race, but as he neared the top of Simpson Hill, he began to get excited about his next bugle lesson. As he rounded the corner of Vermont Street, he did not see Grandpa or his mom on the porch as usual. Scout realized they weren't there, too, and stayed close to the bike all the way to the house.

When he got to the porch, he parked his bike and went in through the back door, announcing, "Hey, I'm home… where is everyone?" Dale thought it was strange that the house was so silent. He peered into the living room and saw Grandpa, Grandma, and his mom all sitting quietly on the large brown leather sofas. "What are you doing inside? Is something wrong?" Dale asked nervously.

His mother stood and slowly began, "Well, it's about your dad."

Dale interrupted, "Is he OK? What happened? Was he hurt at war?"

Dale's mom smiled and replied, "No...." And she glanced to the far corner of the living room, "In fact, he is standing right behind you."

Dale spun around to face his dad. He could hardly believe his eyes.

"Come over here and give me a big hug," his voice boomed.

Dale had not seen him for over a year. Tears welled up in his eyes as he fell into his dad's arms. Scout, after hearing Dad's voice, broke through the screen door so he could be a part of the excitement. With Dale and Scout jumping on him all at once, they all toppled to the floor. Dale continued to give him long overdue hugs while Scout licked him on the face.

Finally, Dale's mom urged, "Jake, why don't you get up so we can have lemonade on the porch."

Dale grabbed Scout by the collar and led the procession to the porch. He sat next to his dad with Scout at his feet, which is exactly where they used to sit before Jake went off to war.

Jake said, "Your mother tells me you and Grandpa have been doing some exciting things the last few days.

Dale answered, "We have," but before he could finish, Grandpa slowly stood up, "Let me show you what I bought for you today Dale." He pulled a small book from his pocket. "I went down to Hamm's Music Store after work and picked this up for you."

Dale took the book from his grandfather's hand and read the title, *The Complete Instructive Manual for Bugle, Trumpet, and Drums.* "Wow! This is great," Dale gently opened the book.

"I think you're old enough to have a real book to play from instead of having to write all of the notes and calls out on paper. This is a book that the military buglers use these days, and it shows you exactly how to play the bugle. The musical exercises are all written out for you to practice. It will help you develop the skills you need to play all of the bugle calls, plus it has all the words to those calls. From now on, I will be able to assign you pages and exercises to play."

Dale couldn't wait to show his friends and Mr. Walsh at the fire station.

Dale jumped up and gave Grandpa a big hug. He thought for a moment and then asked, "Do you remember last night when you explained the words to *Taps* and how they were meant to remind us to enjoy every minute of every day? With Dad coming home and all the things that have happened today, I am really enjoying the day."

"I think we all are enjoying today," Grandpa added. "Now let's have some of that lemonade and hear about what your dad has been up to for the last year and a half."

Chapter 11

DOGS FOR DEFENSE

Mom, Grandpa, Grandma, Scout, and Dale all sat on the porch as Dad talked about everything that had happened since he left for the war last year as an Army Ranger. As he told all of the stories, the family hung on every word. He finally got to the last adventure that explained why he was home and not in the South Pacific fighting.

Dad began, "I want to tell you why I'm home. I was wounded in a battle on the island of Peleliu. I've been in the hospital for the last month recovering, and now I'm on medical leave for the next two weeks before I go back. My wound was not too bad, so your mom didn't tell you, Dale, because she didn't want to worry you...

but I think you need to hear about how a dog just like Scout saved my life."

Dale raised his eyebrows in amazement as his dad patted Scout. "Let me tell you about it."

Dale's father leaned back and began the story. "Each military unit has dogs that help the soldiers. The dogs guard the military bases at night, run messages back and forth during battles when the radios don't work, help sniff out the enemy where they are hiding, and even carry ammunition during a battle. But one of the most important jobs they have is to help find soldiers who are lost or hurt."

"Well, one afternoon several months ago, my company of soldiers was in the thick jungle doing some scouting of enemy positions when we were attacked. As the battle raged on, our platoon got separated from the rest of the company. Several members of my platoon had been wounded and were unable to go any further. I volunteered to get help, but on the way back, I was shot by a sniper and pinned down by enemy fire. I lay still on the jungle floor with fighting going on all around me. After about an hour of fierce battle, I heard a noise in the weeds and thought that this was it—I was either going to get shot or be captured. I was ready for a fight when the weeds parted. Instead of enemy soldiers, Rex, our rescue dog, appeared crawling on all fours. My company had sent Rex to find me and lead me back to them or carry a message indicating my location."

Jake continued, "Rex had a pack on his back with medical supplies and water that I used to patch my wounds. Once I had fixed myself up, I told him to find the unit. Rex carefully led me back through enemy lines, stopping and sniffing so that we avoided the enemy. It took us three hours of crawling and hiding, but we finally reached the company. I never felt so glad to see anyone in my life as my buddies raced to lift me onto a stretcher."

The family sat in silence as Dad finished the story. "Rex was sent back into the jungle to locate the other men who were hurt. That one dog saved four wounded soldiers that afternoon. If it hadn't been for Rex, I wouldn't be here today."

Dad paused to take a sip of his lemonade and looked for a long while at Dale. "They have a program to get more dogs for the military called *Dogs for Defense.* Civilians can donate their dogs to be trained and help soldiers just like Rex did for me. You might think about volunteering Scout for *Dogs for Defense*. The military needs good dogs. Rex saved my life and perhaps Scout could save another boy's father's life."

Dale looked down at Scout and then back at his dad. "I don't know about that..." and his voice trailed off. He touched his dad's hand, changing the subject. "Dad, I'm so glad you're home for two weeks."

Grandma stood up and announced, "Let's have one of your dad's favorite meals, spaghetti." She turned to lead the family into the dining room.

Dad put his arm around Dale as they opened the screen door. "Come on, let's eat—I'm starved."

Chapter 12

SATURDAY

The next morning when Dale woke up, he thought of the stories his dad had told. He had lots to tell his friends. When he came downstairs for breakfast, he was surprised to see Grandpa having a cup of coffee at the kitchen table.

"Are you home because Dad's here, Grandpa?" Dale asked.

"I'm taking today off because tomorrow I have to take a freight train all the way to Chicago and back," Grandpa explained. "Maybe after breakfast, we can have a lesson in your new book before you go to the movies and play in the wooded lot by Charlie's house."

"You mean the Jungle?" Dale corrected.

Grandpa laughed, "Ah, yes...the Jungle.

Dale was excited about the stories he could tell his friends about his dad, but he was also excited about the prospect of a lesson. "Let's eat fast, so we can get started. Can I have half a cup of coffee with cream and sugar like we always do when you're home for breakfast?"

"Yes," Grandpa answered, "but remember, you can only drink it when I'm here. You know your mother doesn't really like me giving you coffee."

Dale poured the coffee into his cup, stirring some cream and two scoops of sugar round and round. He took a sip and sighed, "I really like coffee."

Grandpa smiled, "All good Swedes like their coffee."

Dale plucked a cinnamon rusk from the plate on the table. Both Dale and Grandpa shared a love of this crispy, dried toast. He spread butter on the top and dunked it into his coffee, just long enough to make it moist but not soggy. Dale slowly raised the toast to his mouth and took a big bite. The butter and cinnamon combined with the coffee tasted so good that he ate three more before announcing, "I think four rusks are my limit."

"Let's go have a lesson."

As they walked into the living room Grandpa explained, "I will assign several lessons for you in your new book so when I'm gone, you can continue to practice even with your dad home." Grandpa sat in his big brown leather chair as always and Dale's chair was set next to him. The bugle was on the seat and the new book on a music stand. It was obvious that Grandpa knew Dale would want a lesson. Dale picked up the bugle and slid into the seat.

Grandpa began, "Let me hear you buzz your lips."

Dale buzzed long tones first and then attempted several lip slurs back and forth.

"Good job," Grandpa said. "Now let's do the same thing with the mouthpiece."

Dale put the mouthpiece in the bugle and played the same long tones and lip slurs on the bugle.

"Excellent! Now how about working on the exercise with the notes we wrote out last week."

Dale got out the staff paper with the exercise Grandpa had written out and began to play while Grandpa counted out loud, keeping the beat steady.

"Good," Grandpa said. "But don't forget to keep your air steady for all the beats."

Dale tried again, this time concentrating on keeping the air steady. He proudly set the bugle on his knee as Grandpa turned to "Exercises for Beginners."

Pointing to the notes on the staff, Grandpa asked, "Do you see that there are only five different notes?"

"You mean I only have to learn five notes?"

"Yes. You can play any song on the bugle with these five notes; each song has the notes arranged in its own order and has its own rhythm pattern. When you learn to play the cornet, however, you will have to learn to play all of the notes. You already can play three of the five for the bugle. Do you want to learn to play the other two?"

Dale eagerly nodded his head. He had already learned more than half the notes on this instrument.

"Now play low C, which is the first note below the staff," Grandpa instructed.

"What is the line through the C for, Grandpa?

"That's called a ledger line, which lets you add notes that are lower or higher than notes already on the staff. I like to think of it as a temporary extra staff line."

Dale tried to play C but G came out instead. He furrowed his eyebrows in frustration.

"That's OK," Grandpa encouraged. "Just relax your lips and keep a steady stream of air going. Dale did as he was told, and this time a C came out. "Good! Now play it again and hold the note for at least eight counts. You play and I'll count."

Dale started the note but when Grandpa got to number four, Dale started turning red so he stopped and gasped for air.

"You'll be able to hold the notes longer with more practice," Grandpa said. "Now let's work our way up to the new note, high G."

Dale played the G in the staff on purpose and could hold it out for five counts.

Next he played the C above the G in the staff, which he could hold out for six counts.

Grandpa clapped his hands. "OK, now let's go for the E above the C." Dale remembered he needed to tighten his lips and keep his air steady to reach the higher notes. He took a deep breath, buzzed into the mouthpiece, and out came a high, clear note he did not recognize.

"Wow!" Grandpa exclaimed. "You just played the new note, high G."

"Are you sure?" Dale asked.

"Yes, I'm sure. Try the E again, but remember what the E sounded like and how tight your lips were when you practiced it before. That feeling should be the same every time you play. Once you remember it, you will be able to repeat the note easily. Dale imagined how E sounded and how his lips felt before he played the note. This time he played the E he was sure, because he remembered what it sounded like.

"That was much better," Grandpa announced. "Now let's get the high note you had earlier, the G. Do you remember what that felt like and sounded like?"

"I sure do," Dale replied, and he gave it a try. The sound that came out was full and clear, but he could only hold it for three counts.

"Nice sound," Grandpa said as he leaned over to turn the page. "Don't worry about how long you can hold the G while you are still building lip strength. Here's an exercise I want you to play every day to make your lips stronger."

"Playing long tones does two things. First, it builds strength and second, it develops good tone. The tone or sound you make must always be solid and round, without any edge. Do you remember Aunt Sally?"

Dale was confused about why Grandpa was asking about an aunt he hadn't seen in years. He answered hesitantly, "Yes…"

"Well, she had a real edgy tone to her voice that you could hardly stand to listen to. You surely don't ever want to sound like her," Grandpa said, laughing at his own joke. Dale smiled and pointed at the symbols under the notes, "What are these for?"

"One's called a *crescendo* and the other a *decrescendo* mark. The first one means to gradually get louder and the second means to gradually get softer. You play it like this." And Grandpa took the bugle and demonstrated. He started a note softly, then slowly crescendoed, getting louder and louder until Dale finally put his hands over his ears. Then Grandpa reversed the process and the note started to get softer and softer, so Dale uncovered his ears. The note finally was so soft Dale could hardly hear it.

Dale clapped his hands excitedly.

"Thanks," Grandpa said as he handed Dale the bugle. "But did you hear how I always kept the tone round and the air steady while I got louder and softer? If you want to be a good bugler, you must do this correctly every day."

Dale started on the note G, and as he tried to get louder, the note shifted too high, hitting the C above the staff. Grandpa shook his head.

"Don't tighten your lips as you get louder. Just move more air through the horn, and leave your lips the same," Grandpa encouraged.

Dale tried the crescendo again. This time he got a little louder, but when he tried the decrescendo, he had trouble getting softer.

"Don't worry. Keep practicing these exercises on G until I get home in a couple of days."

Grandpa was anxious to get to the next part of the lesson. "Tonguing is very important for a bugler because it separates the notes and makes them crisp and clear. To tongue correctly, say the sound *ta* or *tu*. You decide which one is best for you. Try saying them."

Dale said *ta* several times in a row. Then he tried the *tu*. "I like the *ta*, Grandpa."

"My motto is, 'If you can say it, you can play it.'" He added, "Make the *ta* sound when you start the note." Dale tried, but a really strange sound came out at first.

"Let me demonstrate," Grandpa said. Taking the bugle he played several notes, tonguing each one so Dale could hear what proper tonguing sounded like. "OK, now you try it again." He handed the bugle back to Dale.

After four or five times, Dale finally got his tongue and the sound to go together like Grandpa's.

"That's a good start, Dale," Grandpa said as he marked the tonguing exercises on the next few pages. "Let's learn about the three types of tonguing." Grandpa pointed to the *Mess Call*. "This call has two of them: single tonguing and triple tonguing."

"Single tonguing is what you just did when you said one *ta*." Grandpa pointed to Exercise #4 on the page.

"Next comes double tonguing. For this you say two different sets of syllables. *Ta* followed by *ka*. Try saying the *ka* sound and put your hand in front of your mouth. You want the same amount of air to hit your hand for each syllable so the notes will have the same sound when they come out."

Dale put his hand up to his mouth and pronounced, "Ta ka."

He looked over at Grandpa with a smile. "You're right! I can feel the air hitting my hand; but they weren't the same. I need to use more air on the *ka* sound."

"Practice saying the two syllables by starting slowly and gradually speeding up, saying one syllable after the other until you can't go any faster. Then stop and start over. It's a tongue twister, so you'll have to practice just saying it. Playing it on the bugle will come later."

Dale placed his tongue behind his teeth and slowly began to get faster.

"Ta—ka—ta—ka—ta—ka—ta—ka–ta–ka–ta–ka–ta–ka–ta–ka–ta–ka–ta–katakataka."

"Good—once you have little or no space between the syllables, keep it steady," Grandpa urged.

Dale tried again. This time he kept the syllables steady until he could continue no longer.

"Remember, don't worry about playing notes, just say them, Dale." And he showed him this exercise:

ta ka ta ka ta ka ta ka ta

"The last type of tonguing is my favorite, triple tonguing. Just say three syllables, two *ta*'s followed by one *ka*. Try saying *ta-ta-ka* once."

Dale repeated, "Ta—ta—ka."

Grandpa leaned toward Dale. "Keep the same amount of air going on each one. Try it again."

Dale said it slowly but could not say it very fast.

"It will come. Do the same thing you did on the double-tonguing exercise. Start slowly and gradually speed up until you can't go any faster."

ta ta ka ta ta ka ta ta ka ta ta ka ta

As Dale wrinkled his brow, and pronouncing the words as fast as he could, he looked up to see his father standing in the doorway smiling. Dad walked over and tousled Dale's hair, saying, "You have the best teacher in the world. I wish I could have played an instrument."

Dale sat up proudly—beaming. Just then the big grandfather clock in the hallway chimed one time, startling Dale. He looked up to see that it was 9:30 and he had to meet Charlie at 10:00 a.m. sharp at the firehouse.

"I promised Charlie and the gang we'd meet before we go to the movie. We're going to see *They Died with*

Their Boots On about General George Custer and the Battle of Little Big Horn."

"That's neat, Dale. I read about the Battle of Little Big Horn when I was your age. A cavalry unit fought in the battle."

While Dale and his father discussed the battle, Grandpa began writing out Dale's practice schedule and a list of pages to study. After he finished, he advised, "Make sure you write down how long and what you practiced. That way I can measure your progress and compare it to the amount of time you practice. You can't get good at anything if you don't track your effort and your progress toward your goals."

Dale nodded and promised he would.

Grandpa and Dad smiled. "You'd better get going to the firehouse. I'll see you in a few days when I get back from Chicago," Grandpa said as Dale gave them both a smile and ran out the door to meet his friends.

Chapter 13
A DAY OF FUN

Dale slid his bike to a stop next to Charlie, Tommy, Dave, Bobby, Victor, and Karl at the fire station as planned.

"Hey, Dale, what took you so long?" Charlie asked.

"I had a bugle lesson with my grandpa, and we lost track of time."

Charlie's dad came out of the fire station and said, "Hey, Dale, what's this I hear? Your dad is home from the war?"

"He's home for two weeks, and I'm sure he would want to have you come by the house and visit before he goes back. He has some incredible stories about the war and a dog like Scout saved his life."

"I'll make sure I come by before he leaves. We sure miss him around here," Mr. Walsh said. "How are those bugle lessons coming?"

"They're great, Mr. Walsh," Dale said. "I even found the words to the *Fire Call*. I'll bring the book by next week and show you."

"That would be great," Mr. Walsh replied as he turned to go back inside. "I've got to work on the back-up generator for the siren. You boys had better get moving if you're going to get to the movies on time."

The boys jumped on their bikes and took off down the street to the Orpheum Theatre. The Orpheum was a theater on Main Street with a large, ornate, triangular marquee that jutted out over the sidewalk. The boys parked their bikes in the rack on the side. As they walked toward the ticket booth, Dale spotted Bridget and Chrissy in the long line that stretched down the block. He asked if they could cut in line with them.

Bridget said shyly, "Sure." And the boys crowded into the small space in the middle of the line, much to the dismay of the other kids standing beside them.

Chrissy turned to the boys beside her. "I hear this is a great movie. I just love Olivia de Havilland and Errol Flynn."

"The last movie I saw with Errol Flynn was called *Dive Bomber*," Victor said. He spread his arms, made a buzzing motor sound, and ran in a circle around the group. Everybody laughed. Finally, the line started moving. As they neared the ticket booth, Dale fumbled in his pocket to retrieve a dime.

"I can't believe they raised the price of the ticket to 10 cents," Dave whined. All the kids agreed as they laid their money on the counter, grabbed their tickets, and herded into the theater.

The cool blast of the lobby air conditioning greeted them. Dale thought of how Grandpa would take Grandma, Mom, Charlie, and him to the movies on hot summer nights just so they could be cool for a few hours. After buying some popcorn and candy, the boys filed into a row near the front. Dale scrambled in after Charlie. As he settled back in his seat, he turned to see that Bridget was sitting next to him, brushing his arm as she laid her arm on the armrest. Dale smiled as the lights of the theater dimmed.

The darkened theater was full of kids who yelled and screamed until the screen lit up. Then everyone was quiet as the newsreel sputtered to life on the screen before the featured movie began. Newsreels relayed information about the war and the events that were happening around the world. On the screen appeared a soldier leading a dog that was wearing a backpack. The announcer stated, "Every day, dogs help soldiers guard our military bases."

Dale turned to Charlie and whispered, "A dog just like that one saved my dad's life."

Charlie shook his head in disbelief.

"I'll tell you about it later," Dale added. "It's amazing."

The film showed dogs in combat, dogs sniffing for land mines, and dogs carrying messages behind enemy lines. "Everyday citizens can help our soldiers by donating their dogs to *Dogs for Defense*." The booming voice of the announcer went on to explain that the military needed over 125,000 dogs for the war effort. "Donate your dogs to *Dogs for Defense* and do your part as an American citizen," the announcer pleaded as John Philip Sousa's patriotic march, *American Patrol*, played in the background.

The screen went dark and Dale's thoughts turned to Scout. Dad had said Scout would make a great military dog just like the ones on the screen. Before Dale had time to consider the idea further, the feature film title flashed on the screen, *They Died with Their Boots On.* Bridget leaned over, her hair lightly touching Dale's shoulder, and whispered, "If I get scared, can I hold your hand?" Dale nodded, and watched wide-eyed as the opening scene panned the plains of the American West.

Soon the screen was filled with cavalry soldiers and Indians fighting. Dale watched intently as a bugler played *Charge* after the troops lined up to go into battle. During the final massacre scene at Little Big Horn, Bridget gripped Dale's hand so tightly that his fingers began to tingle. When the lights came back on, she quickly released his hand and stood up. Chrissy whispered into her ear and Bridget laughed as they turned to file out of the row. "See you, Dale," she said quietly. Dale watched as her blonde ponytail wagged behind her down the aisle. Just then Charlie elbowed him.

"Hey, Dale, what's up with you?" Even in the coolness of the theater, Charlie, swept up by the excitement of the movie, was sweating. "I'm going to go to the library with my mom and get a book about Custer and his last stand at Little Big Horn. I want to read more about it. Maybe I can share it with our class since we're studying the history of the West."

As the boys walked out of the theater into the sunlight, Dave yelled, "Charge!" Victor added, "Let's get the dogs and some lunch before going to the Jungle."

"What about peanut butter sandwiches at my house?" Charlie offered, as Victor and the others expected he would.

They jumped on their bikes with Karl leading the way, his arm waving in the air like General Custer's. "Charge," he yelled. The boys responded by pretending to ride after a band of Indians. Taking their hands off the handlebars, they shot at the make-believe enemy, riding recklessly through the streets of Libertyville. Arriving at Charlie's house, they all agreed that they would have made great cavalry soldiers and would not have lost the Battle of Little Big Horn.

Charlie's mom served the boys peanut butter sandwiches and cold milk at the kitchen table. The boys gobbled their food in silence. After two sandwiches and two glasses of milk, Dale leaned back in his chair, patted his stomach, and announced to everyone that he could not eat another bite. Just then, a loud burp escaped from Dale's mouth. Mrs. Walsh, who was wiping off the counter, turned in surprise. The boys all laughed and Dale quickly apologized, "Sorry, Mrs. Walsh. It just slipped out."

She smiled, saying, "That's what they all say. By the way, what are you boys doing this afternoon other than eating me out of house and home?"

"We're going to our new fort in the Jungle and to play Capture the Flag," Karl answered.

"OK, just remember to head for home when you hear the factory whistle at 5:00," Mrs. Walsh warned.

"Yes, Ma'm," Charlie said sharply, standing up and saluting his mother like he had seen the Cavalry soldiers do in the movie. Mrs. Walsh narrowed her eyes and then shook her head as the boys ran out the door. Charlie untied Smokey and the group biked over to Dale's house to get Scout.

"Hey, I thought that was a great belch at lunch. I'd give it an 8 out of 10," Charlie yelled to Dale.

Karl chimed in, "That was not an 8. It had to be at least a 9. Didn't you hear how long it lasted?"

The other boys agreed with Karl, so Charlie gave in, saying, "OK, a 9 it is. That's going to be hard to beat."

Scout heard the boys coming and started barking before they rounded the corner. Dale jumped off his bike and untied Scout, who was already play wrestling with Smokey. Off to the Jungle they rode, this time much faster since their lunch had started to settle.

The trail into the Jungle was a narrow dirt path that the boys had made from riding their bikes back and forth to work on the fort every day for the past month. There was a trail that led to the pond where they swam on hot afternoons and another one that went to the rock formations at the far end of the Jungle. The boys would climb up and sit on the limestone cliffs to survey the town and to sun themselves on cooler days. They were the only ones who knew where each trail went, which made it easy to lose other kids who would try to follow them, hoping to find the fort.

The fort was an elaborate one-story wooden structure made of scrap lumber. It had a front and back door and a window on each wall to shoot out of. Best of all, it had a ladder and an escape hatch in the ceiling that could be opened from the inside only. The structure was so sturdy that the boys could climb up on the roof to check out the surrounding area for any enemy who dared to approach. A bushel basket full of dirt clods rested next to the hatch ready to be thrown. These were their "grenades," and when they hit the ground, they burst into bits, creating a cloud of dust "just like" a real grenade. When they were building the fort, Karl hit Charlie in the head with a clod that had rocks in it, and Charlie had to get eight stitches at

Doctor Johnson's. Charlie's mom was angry, so the boys didn't tell her how the accident really happened. They did make a pact, however, to not aim clods at the opposing side's head.

The walls of the fort were camouflaged in branches and vines so other kids would have a hard time finding it. No one was allowed to bring other friends, parents, brothers, or sisters to the fort. The boys had agreed that this was their secret place, and they promised not to give away its location.

They slid to a stop at the door of the fort. The dogs started sniffing in the surrounding underbrush while each boy began his assigned duties. Charlie and Karl gathered more big dirt balls for the grenades. Dale began replacing the dried leaves on the fort with new green ones, and Dave and Victor swept out the inside with an old broom they had found, making sure to knock all the spiders, spider eggs, and cobwebs off the walls and ceiling. Tommy really hated spiders, so he and Bobby were assigned to find sticks that looked like guns. Finding the right sticks was an important part of the game because it made it easier to pretend to be "shooting" at the enemy.

After about thirty minutes, the boys were ready. The fort was swept out, the dirt bombs had been gathered, sticks that looked like guns had been found, and the camouflage had been replaced on the walls of the fort. Everyone, including the dogs, went inside and sat in a circle on the floor to pick teams for the first round of Capture the Flag.

Charlie rubbed his head and made them re-promise, "Don't throw clods at anybody's head, especially mine."

Everyone laughed and agreed. The captains of the two teams had been decided earlier—Dale and Charlie.

Dale suggested, "Let's flip a coin to see who chooses first."

Karl had a penny, so he tossed it in the air. Dale called, "Heads."

Karl whined, "You always call heads. That's not fair."

"I call heads because it's always heads," Dale responded, and sure enough, it was heads. Dale picked first.

"I take Scout." The boys all booed.

"Come on, Dale. Scout always sniffs us out before we can shoot you," Karl complained.

"That's why I picked him first and not you, Karl, because you can't smell anything."

Dave teased, "He may not be able to smell, but he sure smells."

Everyone laughed but Karl. Charlie went next, picking Bobby, who could crawl and hide in the weeds better than anyone else. Dale chose Victor, while Charlie chose Dave. Karl was the last to be chosen. To make up for having Scout on his team, Dale offered that Charlie could have both Karl and Smokey. Tommy placed the flag, an old dishtowel tied to a stick, on the roof of the fort.

Dale took charge. "Don't forget you have to get the flag off the pole before you can say your team wins," he cautioned. "My team will attack the fort first, and Charlie, your team will defend the flag. We'll start the battle in ten minutes, no earlier. We need time to hide and make our plans before attacking. Dave, you whistle when ten minutes is up. Then let the battle begin!" Dale and his team ran about a hundred yards down the trail and sat down to figure out their plan of attack.

Tommy announced, "I've got an idea they won't expect," and he drew out the plan in the dirt with a stick. After some discussion, the boys agreed it was a pretty good plan. Scout barked in approval.

"Let's go," Dale commanded. "Remember no talking. Use only hand signals like the real army uses." Hand signals were a great way to point out the enemy or get everyone to stop, hide, or move a certain direction. The boys knew the signals, having practiced them often. Victor was the lookout, and Dale and Tommy spread out into the weeds surrounding the fort. Dave's whistle pierced the air and the game began. Scout stayed close to Dale. The dog began sniffing anxiously in the grass. Dale knew that meant the enemy was close, so he held up his hand for Victor and Tommy to stop. Crouching down, he whispered to Scout, "Find them." Scout started crawling through the weeds, stopping abruptly at a dense patch of brush. He sat and began wagging his tail.

Dale held up one finger and made a walking signal to Tommy. He then pointed at the hiding place while Scout went from sitting to lying down in total focus on the enemy. As Tommy crawled toward the brush, Karl sprang up to shoot Tommy. Dale saw him first and pointed his "machine gun" stick at Karl, yelling his best double tongue sound, "Ta ka ta ka ta ka." Karl raised his hand, signaling he was dead, and the boys continued to crawl to where Scout was pointing. Bobby realized his hiding place had been discovered when he heard Karl get shot. He started crawling through the grass only to be gunned down by Victor who was waiting for him on the other side of the thicket. Dale signaled to move ahead and patted Scout's head in appreciation for a job well done.

Only Charlie, Dave, and Smokey were left to defend the fort. The plan was to attack one side with dirt balls, while Dale and Scout snuck up from the rear. The boys were crawling through the weeds toward the fort, when Scout stopped and started sniffing the air, looking up in the trees. Dale signaled the boys to stop. Shading his eyes with his hand, Dale spied Dave sitting on an overhanging limb, waiting to shoot them when they passed beneath him. Dale made a hand signal for Victor to stand up, getting Dave to move so Dale could shoot him. Victor slowly crawled forward. When he got under the tree, as he stood up, he heard Dale's, "Ta ka ta ka ta ka." Dave raised his hand signaling he was dead. Frowning, he climbed down from the tree as Dale's team and Scout continued to move toward the fort.

Dale waved his team together and whispered confidently, "Let's put the plan in action. There's only Charlie and Smokey left, so I think we can do this."

The team split up with one group going to the hilly side of the fort, and Dale and Scout crawling to the side of the fort that was next to the muddy creek. Dale could hear Charlie shooting out the front window and he knew he could crawl right up to the back of the fort. Dale could hear a barrage of dirt balls hitting the front walls. He knew Charlie would hide under the window, afraid to get hit in the head by another dirt ball. Now that Charlie was pinned down, Dale made his move. He called Scout to get Charlie and motioned to the open window of the fort. Scout took off, jumping through the opening, landing directly on Charlie. Both Scout and Smokey began licking Charlie's face, while Dale slipped in the window and climbed up the ladder to the roof where the flagpole was. Victor and Tommy were still lobbing dirt balls when Dale poked his head out of the roof top hatch. He climbed on the roof, grabbed the flag and yelled, "Cease fire! Cease fire! We won!"

Victor and Tommy, coming out of the weeds to the door of the fort, echoed Dale, "We won! We won!"

Dale climbed down the ladder into the fort. Charlie was still lying on the floor with the dogs standing over him. "Come on, Smokey! You were supposed to warn me, not lick me. Dale, get these dogs off me, will you?"

Dale grabbed their collars and shooed them outside.

"Wow, that was a great battle," Tommy said as he entered the fort. In the distance the boys could hear the Conn factory whistle.

"Come on, let's get home for dinner. I'm starving," Charlie urged.

The boys were dusty and dirty, but they agreed that the new fort made the battles much more fun. They got on their bikes and took off in different directions.

"Come on," Dale called to Scout as he turned to ride up Simpson Hill. "Tonight is fried chicken and Grandma's special noodles." While he rode, he buzzed his lips high and low, saying the syllables for both the double-tongue *ta ka* and the triple-tongue *ta ta ka*. He was surprised at how much he had improved in one day. It must have been from using the double-tongue syllables as a machine gun sound. With that in mind, as he rode his bike he pretended to be a fighter pilot firing his machine gun using the *ta ka ta ka* sound to shoot down enemy aircraft. When Dale reached the top of Simpson Hill, he could see his mom and dad sitting on the porch reading the newspaper. Scout took off running full speed in hopes that he might get a good scratching if he got there first.

Dale's dad stood up when he saw Scout flying down the sidewalk at full speed. He clapped his hands together, calling, "Where's the good dog?" which made Scout run even faster. Scout bounded up the porch steps into Dad's waiting arms and licked his face. "Well, I guess you've missed me." Scout jumped back down and rolled on his back, looking up expectantly. Dad bent down and gave him a double-handed scratch on his belly.

"There you go, Scout," Dad cooed as Dale climbed the porch stairs. The air smelled of fried chicken.

Mom stood up, looking Dale up and down. "With all that dirt on your face you must have had a good time in the Jungle today."

"It was one of the best battles ever, Mom."

Dad put his arm around Dale's shoulder as he opened the door. "Run upstairs and wash your face and hands. Then during dinner you can tell us all about your day."

Chapter 14
PUTTING IT ALL TOGETHER

When dinner was ready, Dale ran down the stairs and burst into the dining room, all washed up and ready to eat.

"You'd better use your *Mess Call* to round up everyone for dinner," Dad advised. "I'm anxious to hear it, even if you only sing it."

Dale began to sing the words to the *Mess Call*.

As he finished singing, Grandma and Mom marched out of the kitchen with a large platter of fried chicken and a bowl of steaming homemade noodles.

"That's a pretty good imitation of the *Mess Call*," Grandma said, as she wiped her hands on her apron. "I can't wait to hear the call on the bugle when you're ready."

"It won't be too much longer," Dale promised as he sat down at the table.

Grandma loaded up his plate with a pile of noodles and two pieces of chicken. After the family said grace, Dale dug enthusiastically into the noodles, sucking them into his mouth and smacking his lips.

"Goodness!" Grandma scolded gently. "You sure are hungry…. But try not to make that slurping sound. It's not polite."

Dale took a bite of crispy white chicken. He didn't say another word until his plate was almost empty.

His dad noticed. "It isn't very often that you eat without talking, Dale. You must be starved."

Dale put his fork down and patted his stomach. "I *was* starving, but now I can slow down and tell you about my day."

For the next thirty minutes, Dale entertained his parents and grandparents with stories about his adventures, beginning with the cavalry movie and the newsreel about the *Dogs for Defense* program.

"I told you the military needs dogs," Jake reminded his son.

"If you could've seen Scout sniffing out the enemy in the Jungle and jumping through the window of the fort, you'd agree that he would make a great military dog."

Dad answered, "Well, you think about it for a few weeks. Then if you're ready, Mom can call Captain Stonemiller at the recruiting station to see if Scout has the qualifications to get into *Dogs for Defense*."

Looking Dale in the eye, Dad added, "Either way, I'm proud of you for even thinking about sacrificing your dog for the good of the country."

Dale pushed his chair back from the table. "Can I be excused from the dinner table so I can practice before it gets too late?"

Grandma nodded. "You mean '*May* I be excused?' Yes, you may. Your grandpa wrote down what you are to practice in the notebook on the piano bench." Grandma and Mom stood up to clear the table as Dale rushed to the living room.

He opened up the notebook and read Grandpa's lesson assignment. His first instruction was to practice buzzing his lips—high and low—before buzzing into the mouthpiece. Next, Dale had to play long tones, lip slurs and several tonguing exercises on the bugle. As he played, he remembered the round and full sound the bugle made when his grandfather played. Dale worked through each exercise until he had played them all. His lips were still tingling from the high G. That note was the hardest and still needed some work, but at least he could reach it about half of the time.

When Dale finished working on his exercises, he began to practice the *Mess Call.* First he counted the rhythms and then he played each phrase one at a time.

After several tries, he was able to play the three phrases, although he sometimes missed the high G and at other times it sounded pinched. Dale furrowed his brow and thought about Grandpa's advice: "Hear the notes before you play them." Determined, he decided to begin working on the *Fire Call.* He wanted to play the call for Charlie's dad and the other volunteer firemen. Dale remembered to start by working out the counts, so he could learn the rhythms first. The *Fire Call* had a new rhythm: a dotted eighth and sixteenth. Dale went back to the earlier exercises his grandfather had written out and made sure he could remember how to count and play this new rhythmic pattern. He took some staff paper off the desk and wrote the counts out under each note, just like he had done with the *Mess Call.*

Dale practiced saying the note names, then the counts. He was really proud of himself because at last he was able to say the counts without writing them underneath the staff. In his mind, Dale could hear Grandpa say, "A good bugle player never writes the note names under the staff." Dale brought the bugle up to his lips and slowly played the *Fire Call*, laboriously working out the counts and pitches.

After several tries, he began to get the notes and counts together until his mom and dad walked in the room. Dad asked, "What are you playing, son? That's not the *Mess Call*."

Dale replied, "It's a new one, the *Fire Call*. I'm learning it for the men at the firehouse."

Dale sat up tall and proud as Dad continued. "By golly, I think they'll really like that. Does it have words too?"

"It sure does. Do you want to hear them?" Dale read from the *Cavalry Manual*:

To the fire,

To the fire

Go to the fire, take the double time

And if you go a bit too slow,

Or soon begin to tire,

Sarge in charge will fuss you know,

because you'll raise his ire.

"What does 'raise his ire' mean, Dad?"

"It means get him mad. The volunteer firemen will get a kick out of those words, but how does it go with the song?" asked Dad.

"I can't play the *Fire Call* very fast," Dale responded hesitantly.

"That's OK," Grandma added, stepping into the living room and drying her hands on a dishtowel. "Go ahead and sing it for us."

Dale sang, slowly at first, putting the words with the notes.

Dad laughed out loud and slapped his leg adding, "I would love to see the firemen's reaction when you sing the *Fire Call* the first time. I think Joe is going to get the nickname 'Sarge' after the firemen hear the words."

"OK, Dale," Mom interjected. "You have practiced long enough for one night. Off you go to bed."

Reluctantly, Dale put the bugle gently back into the leather pouch. He wrapped his arms tightly around his mom, dad, and grandma. Then he bounded up the stairs, taking two at a time and singing, "To the fire—to the fire."

Chapter 15
DAD GOES BACK TO WAR

Sunday mornings were always special because the family usually ate a big breakfast of pancakes, sausages, biscuits, and rusks. When Dale came downstairs, he was surprised that Dad was dressed in his Army uniform with the black Ranger patch on the sleeve.

"Hey, Dad, how come you're wearing your uniform?"

His father began slowly, "Well, after we have breakfast and go to church, your mom is going to drive me to the train. I have to get back to my men and the war."

Tears welled up in Dale's eyes and he hugged his dad tightly. "When are you coming back?" he asked quietly.

"Well that depends on the enemy, but you can bet I'll get home as soon as I can. Are you ready to have that half-cup of coffee turn into a full cup? I think you're old enough. You'll be the man of the house while I'm gone."

Dale smiled and replied, "A full cup with cream?"

"You bet," replied Jake.

The family sat sipping the hot coffee as they ate the steaming pancakes and sausage that Grandma placed in the center of the table. When everyone was finished, Dale ran upstairs to change into his good Sunday outfit and dress shoes.

When he came back downstairs, Dad said, "Will you look at those pants? The way you're growing, I think it's time for some longer ones."

Dale looked down at his feet, self-consciously lifting his leg to inspect the hem.

"Your mom will take care of that while I'm gone. Let's get going. We don't want to be late for church and Pastor Bob's endless sermon."

Everyone laughed as Jake pushed open the screen door, allowing Mom and Grandma to go out first. The church was two blocks away and the family enjoyed this Sunday ritual. As they reached the sidewalk, Chrissy and her family were just leaving their home and joined Dale's family on the walk to church—parents in front and Chrissy and Dale following a few steps behind.

"I like your dress with all the flowers on it, Chrissy. It reminds me of spring."

"Thanks." Chrissy reached over and held his hand.

Dale blushed and continued walking and holding her hand until his mom started to turn around. Then he quickly let go.

"How are you two doing back there?" his mother asked over her shoulder.

"Fine," Dale murmured and blushed again.

Mom smiled slyly at Chrissy and turned back to the conversation she was having with Mrs. Rule. As they continued walking, more neighbors stopped to say hello to Jake, asking how he was doing and when he was going back. Everyone in town liked Dale's dad and wanted to talk to him before church started.

The bells in the church tower started tolling, signaling the start of the service. Dale's family entered through the ornate wooden door and found a pew near the front. The best part of the service for Dale was singing the hymns, played by Mrs. Vincent his music teacher on the large pipe organ. The organ was so loud that the stained glass windows vibrated. Dale felt surrounded by the organ music as he stood singing the hymns with his family. When the service was over, the congregation filed out of the pews and down the aisle to shake Pastor Bob's hand on the way out.

Pastor Bob grasped Jake's hand firmly. "I hear you're going back this afternoon on the train."

Jake replied, "Yes, I am. I'm leaving Dale in charge while I'm gone."

The pastor patted Dale's head and said, "Well, he's growing into a fine young man—and growing out of those pants too."

The family laughed and Dale blushed as they waved good-bye to Pastor Bob. The walk home was somber as the time neared for Dad to leave. Jake had packed his gear the night before, and it was waiting inside the door when the family entered.

Looking Dale in the eye, Dad said, "Your mom will drive me to the train. I want you to stay here and practice your bugle. Grandpa will be impressed with your progress when he gets back from Chicago." Dale held back his tears and gave his father a hug.

Dad stepped back. "I think you're old enough to shake my hand like a man." He grasped Dale's hand firmly. His father then picked up the army green duffle bag, turned and quickly walked out to the car with his other arm around Mom. Scout ran out from under the porch and jumped on Dad.

Dad put his bag down and scratched Scout's belly. "Scout, I want you to take care of everyone." Scout barked as if to agree. Dale stood watchfully on the porch as his mom and dad got in the car and drove away.

Grandma gently tapped Dale on the shoulder. "Why don't I make you some lunch? Then you can practice."

Dale sat down to bologna sandwiches with a big glass of milk. After lunch he went over the lesson from the night before, adding the new exercises that Grandpa had assigned him. When he finished, Mom entered the front door.

"I could hear you clear down the street. I think you're sounding really good. Maybe it's time to play for your friends."

Dale hesitated. "I don't know. Don't I have to wait to get the OK from Grandpa first?"

Mom replied, "Well, I just saw Mr. Walsh and Charlie down at the fire station on my way home from the train. You could ride over and show them the manual with the *Fire Call* and sing the words."

Dale perked up. "I'll take Scout. He needs a good run."

Dale stuffed the *Cavalry Manual* in his back pocket and gave a whistle for Scout, who eagerly scrambled out from under the porch. Dale jumped on his bike and said, "Come on, boy." Scout took off running, as he knew where to go, followed by Dale. When they arrived, Mr. Walsh and Charlie were sitting in front of the station, enjoying the warm September sunshine and having a bottle of cola. Smokey jumped up and ran to greet Scout.

Charlie offered Dale a soda. While Charlie went inside to get a bottle, Dale sat down next to Mr. Walsh and took the manual out of his back pocket.

"Hey, Mr. Walsh, I can show you the *Fire Call?*"

"Great," he replied, "are you going to play it?"

"No. Grandpa has to give me permission to take the bugle outside." Dale opened the manual and read the words aloud.

Mr. Walsh clapped his hands in appreciation. Charlie came out with Dale's cola and stood behind his father and Dale, looking over their shoulders. "OK, now sing the words," Mr. Walsh encouraged. Dale cleared his throat and started singing:

To the fire, to the fire, go to the fire, take it dou-ble time. And

if you go a bit too slow, or soon be-gin to ti-re, Sarge in charge will fuss, you know, be-cause you'll rise his ire.

"Let's all sing with you, Dale." So Mr. Walsh and Charlie joined in.

After several times through, all three of them were singing the *Fire Call* so loudly and having such a great time that they did not hear the other volunteer firemen come out of the station to watch.

When Charlie, his dad, and Dale were holding out the last note, they were startled when the men clapped.

"We didn't know you could sing, Joe," said Bud, one of the younger volunteers. "Well, it sounds like he still can't sing," another fireman added, which made everyone laugh heartily.

"What are you singing?" Bud asked as Joe started turning red.

"It's the *Fire Call* that's used to call all the soldiers to a fire in an emergency. In the early days of this country, they didn't have sirens like we do today, so they used a bugle instead. I'm just learning to play the bugle, so for now I'm showing Mr. Walsh how the call goes by singing it."

Bud asked, "Can we try singing with you?"

Dale read the words again. He then sang the melody as the men followed along. Finally, they all joined in.

As they sang, some of the men changed the word "Sarge" to "Joe." After awhile, all of the men were using Joe's name instead of "Sarge."

Dale told them that his dad had predicted that Mr. Walsh would earn a new nickname.

Slim suggested, "Let's keep 'Sarge' in the song, and Joe, from now on your new nickname is 'Sarge.'"

Joe shook his head and changed the subject. "Come on. Let's finish cleaning the equipment."

"OK, SARGE," the men answered in unison as they laughed and sauntered into the station.

Joe smiled and turned back to Dale. "Thanks, Dale. I'm looking forward to hearing you play the *Fire Call* on your bugle."

"It won't be long before I'm allowed to take the bugle outside to play for people."

Dale put the manual in his pocket and climbed on his bike. He whistled for Scout. As he rode down the street, he could hear the men singing the *Fire Call*.

Dinner was ready when Dale arrived at home. He washed his hands, ran to the table and sat down.

"How did Mr. Walsh like the *Fire Call*?" Grandma asked.

Dale told Mom and Grandma the story of the men singing together and giving Mr. Walsh the nickname "Sarge."

Mom nodded her head. "Your dad was right. He knew Mr. Walsh would have a new nickname."

Dale continued, "Mr. Walsh wants me to play for them when I'm ready. Can I be excused to go practice?"

"*May* I?" Grandma corrected. "You go and practice while your mother and I clean up."

Dale pushed back his chair and ran to the living room before Grandma could change her mind.

Dale repeated the lesson he had practiced earlier in the day. With all this practicing, he found that he was really getting the hang of playing the two calls.

At last, Mom came into the living rooms and announced, "Enough for one day. Off you go to bed."

Dale gave Mom and Grandma a hug and ran up the stairs. All the practicing had worn him out. His head was full of the sounds and the words from the two bugle calls, and he quickly drifted off to sleep.

Chapter 16

THE HARD WORK PAYS OFF

The next few weeks flew by with schoolwork, races against the girls, battles at the fort, singing at the firehouse, and best of all, practicing the bugle with Grandpa.

When Dale had his weekly lesson after school one day, Grandpa said, "You've been playing a long time now. I want to show you how much you've learned." Grandpa got out the assignment notebook. "Let's look at the dates and times you've practiced over the last six weeks."

Grandpa opened the book and pointed at the first entry they had made.

"Do you remember the first lesson?" Grandpa asked.

"I sure do," Dale replied. "We learned how to buzz, count, and read note names."

"You're right," Grandpa laughed. "But look how fast you learned because you practiced every day on the material I assigned. Now you can play all of the exercises and read the bugle calls on your own. That shows that when you work hard and practice correctly, you can do great things. But remember, Dale, hard work and setting goals is not just for music. It can be applied to everything you want to achieve in life. Learning to play music is one way to learn those skills. Due to your hard work, if you can show me today that you can play the *Mess Call* and the *Fire Call*, I'll let you take the bugle outside and show your friends."

"Really? You mean you think I'm ready?" Dale could hardly contain himself.

"Well, first let's hear you play the calls, and then I'll decide."

To warm up, Dale buzzed his lips and then the mouthpiece. Continuing, he played a few lip slurs and long tones before he announced that he was ready. Grandpa took the manual off the stand and closed the book.

Dale was confused. "How will I play the call if you closed the manual?"

Grandpa looked at Dale solemnly. "One thing you have to remember is that all bugle players must have the calls memorized. Think about it...they are in battle or riding their horses and can't hold or read the music."

Dale swallowed hard and looked at Grandpa. "I think I've played them enough to remember them."

Grandpa said, "Let's hear the *Mess Call* first." Dale licked his lips, made sure the first pitch was correct. Then he started playing.

Dale was surprised that it was easier to play without the music. Instead of worrying about the notes, he could concentrate on the sound and the rhythm.

"Excellent! Now play the *Fire Call*."

Dale looked down and stuttered, "I... I... I can't remember it!"

In a gentle voice Grandpa asked, "Do you remember the words?"

Dale nodded his head.

"Think the words and the rhythms and the notes will come to you."

Dale thought for a minute, saying to himself, "To the fire—To the fire." His face lit up and he said, "I got it!" He placed the bugle on his lips and played the *Fire Call* straight through with no mistakes.

To the fire, to the fire, go to the fire, take it dou-ble time. And if you go a bit too slow, or soon be-gin to ti-re, Sarge in charge will fuss, you know, be-cause you'll rise his ire.

Grandpa sat back and smiled. "You wait here. I have something for you." Grandpa walked over to the trunk they had brought down from the attic the first day he started to learn to play the bugle. He opened it and reached into the bottom of the trunk, feeling with his hands. Then he stood up with something in his hand that Dale couldn't see.

"What is it Grandpa? What did you get from the trunk? Show me! Show me!"

Grandpa sat back down. "In the military, to become a certified bugler, a soldier first had to pass basic training. Then he had to play all the bugle calls for the commanding officer from memory in front of the entire brigade. If he could play all the bugle calls correctly, the bugler was presented with this in front of the other troops at a big ceremony."

Grandpa opened his hand and showed Dale his gold 1st Cavalry pin, a pin with two swords crossed with the number "1" in the middle.

Dale did not know what to say. He only stared at the pin as it glinted in the lamplight.

"Golly, Grandpa. Is this pin the one you wore in the Battle of San Juan Hill with Teddy Roosevelt and the Rough Riders?"

"Yes," Grandpa admitted, and his eyes had a faraway look. "I wore this pin with pride, and I think you've earned the right to wear it. You have shown the ability to work hard and not give up, and you've learned how to play the bugle. I feel that you're growing up to be a fine young man, and have made me, your mom, grandmother, and especially your dad, proud." Grandpa stood up and looked at Dale.

"Stand up and receive your pin with honor."

Dale stood at attention while Grandpa pinned the 1st Cavalry pin on the right side of his shirt, just above his heart.

He eyed Dale up and down. "As a Sergeant Major in the United States Cavalry and with the powers vested in me, I present this pin to Bugler First Class Dale Kingston." Grandpa snapped to attention and saluted, which he held until Dale saluted back. "Congratulations, Bugler First Class Kingston." Grandpa's eyes gleamed with pride.

Dale couldn't say anything. He was so excited that he just gave Grandpa a big hug. "Thanks for the pin and for teaching me how to play the bugle, Grandpa."

Grandpa was quiet for a moment and patted Dale on the back. "No, I have to thank you for allowing me to share a part of my life with you that I haven't shared with anyone else. I have one more item to give you." And with that, Grandpa reached back into the trunk and pulled out a brown leather bag with a big strap on it.

"What's that?" Dale asked.

"This leather pack is what I carried the bugle in when I wasn't playing it. You can use it to carry the bugle around with you when you go out and play for your friends. It will help protect it from getting damaged as you ride your bike and play in the Jungle."

Dale carefully took the leather case from his grandpa.

Grandpa added, "We still have a lot more to learn, but you're good enough to play for others now. Off you go…have a good time."

Dale put the leather pouch with the bugle around his neck. He fondly rubbed the pin on his shirt and gave Grandpa another salute.

"Thanks, Grandpa!" Dale yelled as he ran out the door. He whistled for Scout and jumped on his bike to ride to the fire station.

Chapter 17

FIRST PERFORMANCE

The ride to the fire station took no time at all. Charlie was playing with Smokey as Dale came flying down Main Street with Scout running along beside him.

The volunteers were busy checking the equipment as they did every Friday. They washed the fire engines, checked the hoses, and Mr. Walsh tested the back-up generator for the siren. Dale slammed on his brakes, but before Charlie could say anything about the great skid, Dale yelled, "Hey everybody! I have the bugle, and I can play the *Fire Call*!"

Mr. Walsh smiled and asked, "Can we all sing along?"

Charlie added, "That'll be fun."

All the men, including Slim, Bud, Tim, and Shorty, stopped what they were doing and surrounded Dale as he was getting the bugle out of the case.

"What's that on your shirt?" Slim asked.

Dale stuck out his chest, stating proudly, "This is a 1st Division Cavalry pin that my grandfather gave me for learning to play the bugle."

The men admired the pin. Charlie was especially interested. "Is that the one he wore in battle?"

"Yep," responded Dale. "Give me a minute to warm up."

Dale played a couple of lip slurs and then announced that he was ready. Dale warned the men, "Don't sing the first time I play it. You might mess me up." Everyone laughed. Dale licked his lips and began to play. The notes poured out big, round, and clear.

When he finished, the men clapped. "That was really loud!" Charlie insisted, "I bet you could hear that all over town."

"One more time, Dale, and then we'll sing with you," Mr. Walsh added.

"Charlie, you count off 1-2-3 and I will start on 4 so that everyone knows when to start singing. Don't go too fast because I can't play it that fast yet."

Charlie counted off and the men started to sing the *Fire Call* as Dale played.

To the fire, to the fire, go to the fire, take it dou-ble time. And if you go a bit too slow, or soon be-gin to ti-re, Sarge in charge will fuss, you know, be-cause you'll rise his ire.

When they finished, they all clapped. Shorty said, "We should form a fireman's chorus. We aren't half bad."

"We'll think about it," Mr. Walsh answered, turning to resume work on the generator. "I want to get this done before dinner."

"I can play the *Mess Call* also."

Mr. Walsh smiled, "Go ahead, while we go back to work."

Dale played the *Mess Call*, and Charlie sang loudly.

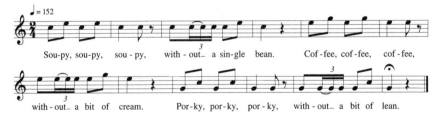

Sou-py, sou-py, sou-py, with-out a sin-gle bean. Cof-fee, cof-fee, cof-fee, with-out a bit of cream. Por-ky, por-ky, por-ky, with-out a bit of lean.

"That makes me hungry," Bud said, rubbing his large stomach. Joe teased, "If you don't get this work done soon, we'll all miss dinner."

"Ok, Sarge," Bud grumbled shuffling back to the fire engine. The men laughed at Joe's new nickname.

Dale turned to his bike and put the bugle in the leather case for the ride home. "Come on, Scout. We'd better get home for dinner."

Charlie reached down and patted Scout's head. "Can you teach me how to play?" he asked.

Dale promised to give him a lesson, then jumped on his bike and rode down Main Street. As the wind blew his hair, he thought with pride about how he had been able to play in front of other people without messing up. The weeks and weeks of practice had paid off. Once he reached the top of Simpson Hill, he could see Grandpa on the porch reading the paper. Dale couldn't wait to tell him about his first performance. Scout bounded ahead for his expected scratching, and Dale raced after him.

When Dale reached the porch, Scout was already on his back getting his belly scratched. Grandpa looked up. "Well, how did it go?"

Dale stood up proudly. "I didn't make any mistakes. All the firemen sang along with me."

Grandpa smiled. "Why don't you get the bugle out and play the *Mess Call* before dinner?"

Dale took out the bugle, licked his lips and pointed it at the screen door. He began to play. When he finished, Grandma and Mom peered out of the door. "Dale, was that you or your Grandpa?" Mom asked.

"It was me. What do you think?"

Mom came onto the porch and tousled Dale's hair. "I think that bugle can be heard all over town," she added.

Chrissy yelled out of her bedroom window that faced Dale's house, "That was great! Play another song."

Dale blushed and played the *Fire Call*.

"Wow! I'll bet you can hear that all over town," she laughed.

"Thanks," Dale yelled back.

"Let's put that bugle away and eat," Grandma urged as she went back into the kitchen. "I think that tonight you and Grandpa can finally do the dishes, after getting out of that chore for the last two months."

Grandpa winked at Dale and stood up. "I knew it wouldn't last forever."

Grandpa opened the screen door and Dale took his hand as they went inside to eat dinner and talk about what a great day it had been.

Chapter 18

THE CALM BEFORE THE STORM

During the next several weeks, Dale learned several more bugle calls. First he learned *Charge*, a call that the boys had heard in movies when the cavalry was ready to attack.

Then he learned *First Call*.

All the boys knew *First Call*. When they went to the horse races at the State Fair every summer, the bugler played *First Call* to signal for the horses to come to the track for the race.

The last call he learned to play was *First Cavalry*, which Grandpa said was the way a division was summoned by their commander. When the commander wanted the First Cavalry, he would play that call. If he wanted the Fourth Cavalry to come, he would play *Fourth Cavalry*. It was an easy way to get the different divisions to come when needed.

Dale played his bugle at the fire station every chance he had. He also brought it to the Jungle and played. One Friday afternoon in Mrs. Vincent's music class, Dale told the class about the bugle and played it for them. He explained how he learned to play from his grandfather, who had been in the cavalry with Teddy Roosevelt. Dale played several calls for his classmates. As he was playing, Mr. Jeffrey, the band teacher, entered the door behind Dale and listened quietly.

When Dale finished, the students clapped. Mr. Jeffrey stepped forward and put his arm on Dale's shoulder. "Where did you learn to play the bugle like that?"

Dale explained that he had been disappointed about not being able to start in the band, so his grandfather taught him the bugle.

Mr. Jeffrey responded, "All I can say is he has done a superb job of teaching. You should be very proud of yourself."

The students clapped again, and then Mrs. Vincent announced, "Please get in line to go back to Mrs. Cooper's class for the last half hour of school."

Mr. Jeffrey shook Dale's hand. "Keep up the good work."

As Dale put the bugle back in the case, Bridget and Chrissy ran over to him. "That was mighty fine, Dale," Bridget said as she flipped her golden hair off of her shoulder. She added brightly, "But don't go thinking you're going to beat us today after school. You do remember it is Friday and that we always race on Friday."

Dale smiled, "How can I forget with you two to remind me?"

They laughed and walked back to Mrs. Cooper's class before the bell rang at 3:30. As they slid into their seats,

Principal Prenty announced over the loudspeaker, "I would like all of the students and staff to please keep an eye on the weather. Severe storms could be coming our way."

Mrs. Cooper added, "If it gets any darker, you should hurry home and not stay outside playing."

All the kids ran to the window and looked at the dark clouds off to the west.

Charlie said, "That doesn't look that bad. I say we still have the race."

Everyone agreed, and when the bell rang, they headed out to the track. The air was hot and muggy. There was not a whisper of wind.

Bridget looked intently at the sky. "It's really hot and kind of spooky quiet." Charlie mopped his forehead with his handkerchief. "Does that mean you don't want to race today?"

Bridget shook her head and pulled her blonde hair into a ponytail with a rubber band.

Dale looked at the sky. "It's really getting dark. Let's hurry up and get this race going."

Dale, Charlie, Tommy, Dave, Bobby, Victor, Chrissy, Bridget, and Karl all walked faster.

Tony, the seventh grader who was the official judge, ran up and warned, "Come on. It looks bad out."

The boys and girls got down in starting position and waited for Charlie to start the race.

Charlie raised his arm. "On your mark, get set," and just when he was ready to say "Go," a huge bolt of lightning came down, immediately followed by a loud clap of thunder.

The kids looked up at the sky and froze.

In the distance, Mr. Jeffrey came out of the school and yelled, "You'd better get home now. This is going to be a big storm." Just then, raindrops began to fall.

"Come on, let's get home," Dale said as they all ran back to the bike rack. Bridget and Chrissy had walked to school and were really scared. Dale comforted the girls, "Don't be scared. Charlie and I can ride you home on the seat of our bikes if you want."

Charlie offered to take Bridget on his bike.

Dale turned to Chrissy and asked, "I have to go to the firehouse and pick up Scout first. Is that OK with you?"

"Sure," she said as she glanced back up at the darkening sky. "Let's hurry."

Dale swung his leg over his bike, and then Chrissy slid up on the seat behind him. She put her arms around his waist under the leather bugle bag. Dale took off riding as fast as he could. Charlie was right behind him with

Bridget clutching him for dear life. The ride to the fire station only took a few minutes, and when they arrived, they went inside.

Charlie yelled, "Dad, where are you?"

Mr. Walsh answered, "Back here by the generator."

The children gathered around him as he bent over the generator.

"I'm checking the generator just in case we lose power. It's been acting up lately, so I wanted to check it one more time." Mr. Walsh looked up at Dale. "You'd better get Scout and head home. Your mom will be worried and so will Chrissy's. Charlie, you throw your bike in the back of the truck, and I'll drive Bridget home."

When Dale and Chrissy went back outside, Scout began to pace nervously because of all the thunder. Dale leaned down and patted him. "Don't worry, Scout. You'll be fine if you stay with me." Dale jumped on the bike with Chrissy on the seat.

Chrissy wrapped her arms around Dale's waist. He had to stand up to pedal, which made his leg muscles burn from riding so fast. He noticed the wind had picked up.

As he made his way up Simpson Hill, Dale turned his head to Chrissy. "I think all that racing has made my legs stronger. I'll have you home in no time."

Chrissy leaned her head on his back. "I'm glad I'm with you. You make me feel safe."

Dale didn't answer. He just pedaled harder. When he reached the top of the hill, his legs were burning and tired, but he only had two blocks to go.

"We're almost there," Dale yelled as a clap of thunder echoed in the distance.

They pulled up to Chrissy's front porch, just as the rain began to fall harder. She jumped off the bike, then turned and gave Dale a big hug.

Dale looked down at the ground and said quietly, "I'll always protect you. You're really special."

Chrissy blushed and ran into the house.

Dale heard a porch door slam shut. Grandpa called, "Dale, you'd better come in before the storm hits. We were getting worried about you!"

Dale ran up on the porch with his bugle on his shoulder while Scout scampered under the porch.

Grandpa clapped his hands. "Come on, Scout. Tonight you can come in the house."

Scout ran up the steps, tail wagging, as Grandpa held open the door.

Grandpa looked down Simpson Hill at the town below. "I think we're going to get a huge storm tonight."

He and Dale looked up at the sky. The clouds were now dark purple. The flashes of lighting were getting closer by the minute.

Grandpa asked, "Do you remember how to tell how close a storm is?"

Dale replied, "I sure do. When you see the flash of lightning, you say: *one one thousand one, two one thousand two,* and so on until you hear the thunder. Each time you count to five that means the storm is one mile away. If you count to fifteen, then the storm is three miles away."

Grandpa nodded. Dale added, "That's why I wasn't too scared coming home. I counted to *twenty-five one thousand* after seeing the lightning when I was riding Chrissy home and I knew the storm was five miles away."

"What would you have done if the lightning were only one mile away?"

Dale thought for a moment and answered, "I would've stayed at the fire station until the storm was over."

"Good boy! I like the way you think. Let's get some dinner," Grandpa said as the rain began to fall harder.

Chapter 19

THE STORM

Dale's mother came home a few minutes later and explained that she had stayed late at the Air Force base to make sure the planes were tied down. The weather station in Crawfordsville, about fifty miles west, reported that the town had had a lot of storm damage from high winds.

Grandma carried a platter of roast beef and potatoes to the table. "Enough talk about the storm. Grandpa, can you say grace?"

As Dale wolfed down his dinner, the storm seemed to be passing to the south of town. Everyone relaxed a little bit as the thunder moved farther away. Dale relayed how he had played the bugle for Mrs. Vincent's music class.

Grandpa grinned when Dale told them how Mr. Jeffrey had heard him playing and came into class, congratulating him on how well he was playing. Then Dale told about how the principal had warned the students about the storm and how he rode Chrissy home on his bike.

Mom looked at Dale approvingly. "That was really nice of you to do that. I'm sure Chrissy's mom will want to thank you the next time she sees you."

"May I be excused so I can go out on the porch and watch the storm?"

"Yes, you may," Grandma laughed. "But I want Grandpa to sit with you, and if the weather turns bad, I want you both to come in."

Dale got up from the table. "Come on, Scout. Let's go on the porch." Scout had a mind of his own and just curled up on the rug by the fireplace. "I think Scout is afraid he won't get back in the house if he goes outside."

Grandpa laughed and said, "I think you're right. Come on, I'll go with you."

Dale and Grandpa were outside for about ten minutes when Grandpa asked, "Do you feel that?"

The wind had shifted and suddenly the temperature dropped.

Grandpa explained, "That means the storm front is fast approaching." As he finished his sentence, the wind began to blow even harder and the lightning began to flash across the valley, lighting up the sky.

Dale saw one flash. "One one thousand one, two one thousand two, three one thousand three, four one thousand four, five one thousand five," he counted, followed by a big clap of thunder.

"Won't be long now," Grandpa predicted. "The eye of the storm is only one mile away." When they saw the next flash, they both counted together, "One one thousand one, two one thousand two, three..." and then a sharp boom of thunder.

Grandpa watched the swiftly moving clouds. "Only half a mile away." The gusts of wind were bending the trees. The rain started coming down in sheets. On the next flash of lightning, Grandpa and Dale said in unison, "One one thousand..." and before they could finish, a huge clap of thunder vibrated their chairs, seeming to shake the foundation of the porch.

Just as Dale turned to speak, the power went out. The house went dark. Everything was pitch black, as was the valley below. The only time Dale could see anything was when the lightning flashed, which was almost non-stop.

"Let's light the hurricane lanterns and go down to the basement," Grandpa advised as he stood up. "This is going to be a huge storm." Dale opened the door, met by Grandma and Mom, lanterns swinging in their hands.

Grandpa was impressed. "How'd you light them so fast?"

With a glint in her eye that the lantern picked up, Grandma said, "We lit them about ten minutes ago. We knew the storm would knock the power out, so we planned ahead."

Mom took Dale's elbow. "Come on, Dale. Let's hurry to the basement." As Dale passed the piano bench, he grabbed the leather bugle case, the *Cavalry Manual*, and his lesson notebook. Grandpa leaned toward him and whispered, "I don't blame you for wanting to take your valuables with you." The musty smells greeted them as they made their way down the darkened wooden stairway.

The family huddled in the far corner of the basement. As they sat on the floor against the rough foundation walls, they could hear the wind roaring and the rain beating on the side of the house and basement windows. The lightning flashed and the thunder rolled overhead. The whole house seemed to shake. Several times they could hear tree limbs snapping in the wind and hitting the house. Dale was scared, but he didn't want to show his fear. Scout sat in Grandpa's lap, looking up at the flashes of light in the windows. The storm lasted about thirty more minutes. By then, the rumbling had moved into the distance. Dale cocked his head and listened to make sure the storm was gone.

Scout hopped off Grandpa's lap as Grandpa stood up. "Let's go upstairs and see if we had any damage."

Dale picked up the case and music and followed the lanterns as they went upstairs and out onto the porch. The sky had cleared, and in the moonlight, Dale saw that their two rockers had blown off the porch. Tree limbs littered the lawn and street. The tree in front of Chrissy's house had fallen between the houses, ripped out by the roots from the force of the storm. Neighbors came out of the houses and surveyed the damage.

Grandpa took one of the lanterns and walked around the house to check for damage. "I think we were really lucky to have survived." He and Dale hoisted the chairs and carried them back on the porch.

"Dale, I think you should go to bed now. We'll have a lot of cleanup to do tomorrow." Dale reluctantly went up the stairs to bed, but he was so tired that he fell fast asleep without even changing into his pajamas.

Chapter 20

A CALL TO ARMS

Dale had been asleep for about an hour when he was awakened by Scout licking his face and whining. The house was dark, and there was not a sound anywhere outside.

Dale covered his head with his pillow. "Come on, Scout. Leave me alone!" Scout continued to whine and lick Dale's arms. As he sat up, Dale caught a whiff of something strange. It smelled like something was burning. He went to the window and scanned the valley. In the moonlight, he could see smoke rising from the Conn instrument factory. He rubbed his eyes to make sure that he wasn't imagining things. Why didn't he hear the firehouse siren calling the volunteers? As he stood watching the cloud of smoke grow more ominous, Dale realized that the generator must have failed and that the volunteers were unaware of the fire. Dale ran to his grandparent's room, shouting, "Come look...I think there's a fire at the Conn factory!"

Grandpa jumped out of bed and followed Dale to his room and looked out the window. "Hmm.... I think you're right. Where's the siren?" Grandpa picked up the phone to call the firehouse, but the line was dead. The storm had knocked out the phone lines as well as the power lines.

Dale was anxious. "What should we do? What should we do?" he repeated as he rubbed his hands through his hair.

Grandpa had an idea. "I want you to get your bugle and ride to Charlie's house. Play *Fire Call* at every corner on your way. The sound of the bugle will carry across the town." Dale's eyes lit up and he added, "The volunteers who have heard me play will know that I'm playing the *Fire Call*! Then they'll head to the station."

"Yes," Grandpa encouraged. "Once you see them coming, tell them where the fire is and then keep playing the call until you hear the sirens from the fire engines. Do you think you can do that, Dale?"

Dale swallowed hard and nodded his head.

"Good! Now hurry up and get going. This is going to be your most important performance ever!"

Dale raced down the stairs, took the bugle out of the case, and ran outside. Grandpa and Scout were right behind him.

"Hurry, Dale! You have no time to spare!" Grandpa warned as Dale hopped on his bike. He put the bugle to his lips, but nothing came out.

"Remember what you have been taught," Grandpa said.

Dale licked his lips and tried again. This time *Fire Call* came out loud and clear. The sound echoed across the valley.

Grandpa shouted, "Now ride to each corner and play it as loud as you can."

Chrissy leaned out her window next door and yelled, "What's wrong?"

As Dale turned to ride down Simpson Hill, he called, "There's a fire at the Conn instrument factory!"

"Ride, Dale, ride!" Chrissy's voice faded, as Dale pedaled away down the street with Scout running beside him.

At each corner he stopped and played the call. Finally Dale decided to play as he rode so he could cover a wider area. He had to ride around tree limbs that littered the street, but nothing could stop him from playing the *Fire Call*.

Just as he was passing a modest one-story house, he saw Slim, the fireman, run out, yelling, "What's wrong? You're playing the *Fire Call*. Is there a fire somewhere?"

"Yes," Dale gasped, out of breath, "at the Conn factory. I think there's something wrong with the fire siren."

Slim took off running toward the fire station. Dale continued riding down the street and playing. Bud and another volunteer ran out of their houses when they heard Dale approach. Scout ran up to greet them.

Dale told them about the fire, and they sprinted toward the fire station. Finally, Dale got to Charlie's house as Mr. Walsh was putting on his boots on the front porch. Smokey ran up and sniffed Scout.

"Dale, I heard the *Fire Call*, and I knew something was wrong. Where's the fire?" Mr. Walsh asked quickly.

Dale gasped, "At the Conn instrument factory. I saw it from my window."

Mr. Walsh took off running for the fire station. "Keep playing," he called. "It will wake up the rest of the volunteers."

Scout was barking loudly as Dale rode and played the call.

As he turned the corner, he could see Charlie behind him in the moonlight. Dale squinted to be sure he wasn't seeing things. Sure enough, it was Charlie riding his bike, still in his pajamas, with Smokey following behind. He stopped with a skid to avoid running headfirst into Dale.

"I heard you tell Dad about the fire," Charlie said. His hair was soaked with sweat and his chest was heaving with excitement.

"Come on, Charlie," Dale said. "Let's ride to every corner and then to the firehouse and play from the roof. The sound will carry across the whole town." In the distance, the boys heard the sound of the first fire truck siren. Some of the volunteers must have reached the firehouse and were on their way to fight the fire. Charlie and Dale raced down the street and pulled into the fire station driveway just as Mr. Walsh jumped on the back of another fire truck.

He called to the boys. "Go to the roof and keep playing until the last truck is gone. Hurry!"

Dale and Charlie tore up the stairs to the flat roof. Dale stood near the wall that lined the edge of the roof and began to play. The sound was strong and clear in the cool night air. Charlie's voice, alerting the town to the fire's location, echoed down the streets. The volunteers prepared the last truck and roared off, its siren fading in the distance.

Exhausted, Dale brought the horn down from his lips. He and Charlie sat down on the metal roof and looked toward the smoke that was wafting across the valley. He hoped that the firemen would be able to save the factory.

"Charlie, thanks for helping me wake up the firemen. But do you know how funny you looked riding your bike in your pajamas?"

Charlie looked down at his pajamas and began laughing. "I got so excited, I just ran out of the house. I didn't even think about what I was wearing."

Both boys laughed. Dale teased, "I think I have a nickname for you. It's PJ."

"Come on, Dale! Everyone will laugh at me if you start calling me that."

Dale thought for a moment and then relented, "OK... PJ will just be between you and me."

"Thanks," Charlie said, as they both stood up to go back downstairs. "The gang would really kid me if they knew I rode all over town in my pajamas."

Dale shook Charlie's hand. "You'd better get home and get changed before anyone else sees you."

When they came out of the firehouse, the streets were full of people talking about the fire. With Scout close behind, Dale rode slowly, weaving in and out to avoid running over the blown down tree branches. Even though the power was still out, in the bright moonlight he could see clearly. When he got to the top of Simpson Hill, Dale stopped and looked across the valley at the Conn factory. He could only see smoke and no flames.

"Maybe the volunteers got there in time," he thought as he rode the final two blocks home.

When Scout and Dale rode up, Grandma and Grandpa were sitting on the porch with hurricane lanterns beside them.

Chrissy was sitting with them. "We were worried about you," she said softly.

Grandpa added, "I could hear the *Fire Call* all over town." Dale sat down on the porch next to Chrissy and told them all about it.

Finally, Grandma leaned over and said, "I'm really tired. I think we should all go back to bed."

Chrissy leaned over and hugged Dale tightly. "You're so brave. You saved the factory."

Dale blushed, "What else could I have done?"

Chrissy stood up and said good-bye. She walked back to her house, and Dale and Scout followed Grandma and Grandpa inside.

Dale became aware that someone was missing. "Where's Mom, Grandpa?"

"When she heard the bugle call and saw the fire was near the Air Force base, she drove over to see if she could help. You should've seen her drive that Jeep through the yard to get around the fallen trees. It was quite a sight. I'm sure she'll be back soon. You should get to bed...this has been a long night."

Dale hugged his grandfather tightly. Grandpa patted his head. "You made me real proud, son. Your mom and dad would be proud, too." Grandpa turned to Scout, gave him a big scratch on the belly, and said, "Well we can't forget you Scout because you were the one that smelled the smoke and woke us all up." Scout barked twice and rolled over for another scratch.

"OK, Scout, enough scratching, now off to bed for you two," Grandpa whispered.

Dale fell into bed exhausted, too tired to bother taking off his clothes that smelled of smoke. Within a few minutes, he was fast asleep.

Chapter 21
THE NEXT DAY

Dale was awakened by the bright sun shining through the window. He couldn't remember when he had slept so late. Dale struggled out of bed and stood at the open window. The air still smelled of smoke from the night before, but when he looked across the valley, he couldn't see any smoke rising from the factory. Dale's stomach growled as a reminder he needed to eat, so he hurried downstairs to the kitchen. Mom was sitting at the kitchen table. She had ashes on her face and smelled of smoke. She had just taken a sip from a steaming cup of coffee when she looked up to see Dale.

"Well, look who's finally getting up! It seems like the town hero needs some breakfast and maybe a hot cup of coffee with cream."

"A full cup?" Dale asked.

"Sure, you've earned it. Your Dad said you were old enough even before last night. Wait until he hears about what you did," Mom said, setting down her cup.

"What do you mean the town hero?" Dale probed as he sat down at the table.

"Without you playing your bugle to awaken the town, we would have lost the factory and maybe the Air Force base. That's how big this fire could have been."

"I'm not a hero," Dale looked down into the cup of coffee swirling with cream. "I just did what any bugle player would do."

Grandma entered the kitchen and piped in, "Don't be modest, Dale. The whole town appreciates what you did." She set a plate of rusks on the table.

"Thanks, Grandma." Dale dunked a rusk and shoved it into his mouth. "What happened at the fire, Mom?"

Mother explained, "The fire in the warehouse next to the factory started from a lightning strike. By the time the firemen arrived, the warehouse was completely engulfed in flames. Fortunately, the volunteers got there just in time to keep the fire from spreading to the main factory and the planes we had parked next to the factory fence. The other WASP pilots heard your call and came to help move the planes and fight the fire. Everyone pitched in and saved not only the factory but the planes as well. It was all because you played the *Fire Call* to alert the town." Mom stood up, gave Dale a hug, and excused herself to clean up before going back to the base.

Dale asked, "May I go to the fire station after breakfast and then to the Jungle to check on the fort to see if it's OK?"

"Sure...but be careful. Trees and limbs are down everywhere," Mom warned.

Dale continued talking to Grandma while he dunked his rusks and drank his hot coffee. When he had eaten all the rusks he could, he asked to be excused. Then he whistled for Scout and hopped on his bike. As he rode down the street, neighbors were cleaning up limbs and cutting the trees that had been blown over by the wind. When they saw Dale, people would stop working and wave. "Thanks, Dale!" they shouted.

Even people he didn't know waved and thanked him for saving the factory. By the time he got to the fire station, the fire trucks were returning from the fire. The men's faces were covered with soot and ash. Hopping off the trucks, they began their routine putting all the equipment away.

Slim saw Dale and called to the other men.

Everyone stopped what they were doing and came to the center of the driveway, surrounding Dale. Bud began clapping, joined by Slim and the others. Their smiles broke through their ash-covered faces. Mr. Walsh moved the men aside and stepped into the center of the circle with Dale.

"I need to shake the hand of the young man we are all indebted to for saving the Conn factory and the Air Force base. There can't be a bigger hero anywhere." Mr. Walsh shook Dale's hand vigorously. "You're one special musician!"

The firemen cheered and picked Dale up. They placed him on Mr. Walsh's shoulders and marched him into the firehouse, singing the words to the *Fire Call*. "To the fire, To the fire..."

Once inside, the men sat down and Slim offered Dale a cold bottle of cola. Then each man told his version of how he fought the fire. They all laughed as they told about waking up as if in a dream and hearing the *Fire Call*.

When they finished telling their stories, Dale told them how happy he was that none of them had been hurt in the fire.

"We're glad, too, since it was a really big fire," Mr. Walsh admitted as he stood up. "Come on, men. Let's finish up so we can go home. We've had a long night."

"You heard Sarge. Let's get moving," Slim echoed.

Before he walked out of the firehouse, Dale asked where Charlie was. "Probably at home asleep. Why don't you ride over and wake him?"

Dale jumped on his bike and whistled for Scout who had been playing in the back with Smokey. "See ya later, Mr. Walsh," he called. As he rode down the driveway, he could hear the men singing "To the fire, To the fire" as they put the equipment away.

When Dale arrived at Charlie's house, Charlie's mom greeted him with a big hug. "Here's our hero! I'm so proud of you and Charlie for what you did last night. I've been hearing Joe sing that *Fire Call* for weeks now, so when I heard it in the middle of the night, I knew something was wrong."

Charlie came downstairs rubbing his eyes, still in his pajamas. "That was some night, don't you think?"

"It sure was, PJ," Dale answered and smiled at his friend.

Charlie reddened. "Hey, you promised not to tell anyone about that!"

"I'm sorry," and he reached out to shake Charlie's hand. "You're the best friend a guy could ever have."

"So what happened at the fire?" Charlie asked, relieved that Dale wouldn't tell anyone about his wardrobe the night of the fire.

Dale explained what his mom had told him and what he'd heard at the firehouse and how happy he was about what he and Charlie had done.

Charlie jumped up and down. "Let me change my clothes. Then we can get the gang and see if the fort was damaged by the storm."

"Be careful...there are limbs down everywhere," Charlie's mom added.

As soon as Charlie was dressed, the boys rode their bikes to get Karl, Victor, Tommy, Bobby, and Dave. As they picked up each one on their way to the Jungle, they had to tell the story about fire.

Karl was leading the pack of boys on their bikes. "I could hear you playing clear down at my house. I knew something had happened because you were playing the *Fire Call*."

As they whizzed by, a man yelled, "Thanks for saving the town!"

"Wow!" admired Dave. "Do all these people know who you are?"

Dale shook his head in disbelief at the events of the past twenty-four hours. Never in his dreams had he imagined that he would even be considered a hero.

When the boys arrived at the Jungle, the trail was blocked with trees that had been toppled by the storm.

"Let's leave our bikes here and walk in," suggested Charlie. The boys made their way toward the fort down the muddy trail, stepping over limbs strewn across the path. As they rounded the final curve, they stopped dead in their tracks. No one said a word. The boys just stood silently, mouths open.

Finally, Dave managed to speak. "Do you believe that huge oak tree fell on the fort and crushed it?"

Charlie sat down on a rock and put his head in his hands. "All that work destroyed by one storm."

Dale wasn't willing to give up. "Maybe we can build a better fort in the middle of the blown down limbs." His face brightened as he added, "Then it would be really hard to find."

"Good idea! Let's get started," Karl said as he reached down to pick up some branches.

The boys salvaged as much wood as they could. They began digging and dragging the limbs and wood to the clearing. They were so involved in the task of rebuilding the fort that they didn't hear anyone coming until Charlie turned around and blurted out, "Oh, oh! I think we're in trouble."

Dale stopped dragging a huge log. When he turned around, he was face to face with four stern soldiers in their battle fatigues.

Dale swallowed hard and said, "We didn't mean to do anything. We just wanted to build a fort for fun, and now we're trying to fix the damage from the storm."

The biggest soldier stepped forward and asked crisply, "Which one of you is Dale Kingston?"

The boys looked at each other, afraid to answer.

Finally Charlie stuttered, "It's him, it's him!" and pointed at Dale.

Dale stepped forward. "I'm Dale Kingston. Am I in trouble?"

The tough looking soldier smiled. "We have been sent by General Packston to find you and another boy named Charlie Walsh. Is he here?"

Dave imitated Charlie. "It's him. It's him," pointing to Charlie.

Charlie glared at Dave as he cautiously stepped forward. "I'm Charlie Walsh. Am I in trouble too?"

"I am First Lieutenant Dirk Swenson," the soldier said as he saluted. "The only thing you boys did was save the Conn factory and the Air Force base. I was sent to find you boys and give you these orders to report tomorrow afternoon at twelve hundred hours to the town square to meet General Packston."

Charlie furrowed his brow. "What is twelve hundred hours?"

"That's military time for twelve o'clock noon," one of the soldiers replied.

"But how did you find us?" Dale asked.

"What do you think the Airborne units are trained to do? No one can track people like the Airborne can," Lieutenant Swenson explained. "Now take these orders home and make sure you're on time. The military does not take kindly to people being late."

The soldiers snapped to attention, giving the boys a salute. Dale came to attention and returned the salute. "OK, boys. Resume work."

The soldiers then turned and disappeared into the tall grass.

Victor let out a loud sigh. "They scared me half to death sneaking up on us like that."

Dale looked down at Scout. "I guess they really know how to play army. Even Scout didn't hear or smell them." Then he turned back to the log he had been dragging. "Let's get this done so we can go home. I want to show my mom the orders I got from General Packston."

The boys worked diligently for about another hour until their bodies ached. As they walked back to their bikes, they discussed possible ways the soldiers had been able to sneak up on them.

Before they left for home, Dale suggested, "Why don't we meet at the town square tomorrow at noon or twelve hundred hours?" Everyone agreed and Karl, Dave, Tommy, Bobby, and Victor rode off in different directions to their houses. Dale and Charlie watched them for a moment.

"What do you think will happen tomorrow afternoon?" Charlie said.

I don't know. I guess we'll just see what General Packston has in mind," Dale said. Charlie smiled and rode off with Smokey trailing behind.

Dale swung his leg over the bike and looked at Scout.

"Don't look at me like that. You're the one that didn't smell or hear those soldiers sneak up on us. Some kind of guard dog you are." With that, he pedaled home as fast as he could to show the orders to his mother and grandparents.

Chapter 22

CELEBRATION
IN THE SQUARE

The next morning, Dale in his pajamas sat next to Grandpa at the kitchen table, but he didn't feel too much like eating. The orders he had received from the general lay on the table in front of them.

Grandpa told Dale, "Your dad is a Ranger, and they are the finest soldiers in the Army. It's too bad he's not here to go with us." Mom, who was busily wiping off the counter, urged Dale to wear his Sunday clothes and dress shoes for the meeting with General Packston. Dale gulped his glass of freshly squeezed orange juice and bolted from the table.

When he came back downstairs, Grandma had on the flowered dress that she always wore for special occasions. Grandpa came down wearing his tie and Sunday suit while Mom had on her military dress uniform.

"Why is everybody so dressed up?" Dale asked. "We're just going to meet some general."

Mother looked at him in surprise. "What do you mean, just some general?"

Just then there was a knock at the door. A soldier in dress uniform asked if a Dale Kingston was ready.

Dale's eyes widened. "Ready for what?"

"Come with me young man. The General is waiting," the soldier said crisply. Dale recognized the soldier from the day before at the fort. "I am Lieutenant Buck Jones, my orders are to have Dale ride in the front Jeep with me, and your mother and grandparents will follow in the general's staff car. This way please," he said as he opened the door.

As the soldier escorted the family down the steps of the porch, Dale eyed the two Jeeps and staff car that were waiting at the curb. In the second Jeep, Charlie sat with a huge smile on his face and waved.

The first Jeep did not have any doors or top. Four soldiers were packed in the backseat or sitting on the back edge. Dale hopped in and turned to the soldiers, "Hi! I remember you from yesterday."

They smiled and said, "Welcome aboard, Sir." The lieutenant swung his legs in and the engine of the Jeep rumbled to life. With a jerk, the procession of military cars moved down the street toward the town square. The wind and the sound of the engine were even more exciting than Dale could have imagined. They turned onto Main Street and headed west toward the courthouse. As they rounded the corner of the town square, Dale saw hundreds of people in front of the large white bandstand in the center of the square.

Dale turned to the lieutenant and said, "I thought we were going to meet the General? Why are all these people here?"

Lieutenant Jones stared silently ahead and whipped the Jeep around so they were facing the bandstand.

The soldiers hopped out and one of them strode up to Dale's door. "Sir, the General requests that you join him on the bandstand." Dale jumped out and the soldiers saluted.

Dale looked over at Charlie who was standing with his mouth open, surveying the crowd. "Come on, Charlie. Let's go see."

The two boys, their parents, and grandparents climbed the steps. The band began playing *Star and Stripes Forever* by John Philip Sousa.

Charlie whispered, "I know this song."

When Dale and Charlie got to the top of the stage they came face to face with a tall tanned soldier. His uniform was covered with medals and braids. Both boys stopped and stared at the soldier who towered over them. The General extended his hand to the boys and their parents.

"Hello, I'm General Packston. It's my pleasure to meet you two fine young men and your families. I'll be introducing you to the people who want to pay their respects to you for the heroic efforts you made to save the Conn instrument factory and the Air Force base."

The General turned toward a white-haired man standing next to him. "I want you to meet Mr. Carl Greenleaf. He's the owner of Conn Instruments, one of the finest makers of musical instruments in the world."

Mr. Greenleaf came forward and vigorously shook each boy's hand. He continued down the line shaking the hand of each family member.

"Next, I want you to meet Mr. Joe Maddy, the president of the National Music Camp at Interlochen, Michigan." Mr. Maddy stepped forward, shaking their hands and saying, "I hear, Dale, that you're a great bugle player. I was having dinner last night with Mr. Greenleaf when we heard about the fire and how you alerted the town." Dale looked over at Grandpa, who winked at him in encouragement.

Finally, the General introduced the families to the mayor of the town who couldn't thank the boys enough for what they had done.

General Packston strode over to the podium, waiting for the band to finish before tapping on the microphone and clearing his throat. Dale looked down at the audience. He could pick out his teachers, Mrs. Cooper, Mrs. Vincent, and Mr. Jeffrey, smiling up at him.

"I would like thank Edwin Franko Goldman and his band for playing today." The General turned toward the band and began clapping. He turned back and said, "Let me begin today by saying that we are here to honor two fine young men, Dale Kingston and Charlie Walsh. They represent what America is about."

Charlie leaned over to Dale and asked, "Is he talking about us?"

Dale nodded and gazed at the hundreds of people in the audience. He looked for his friends and at first he couldn't find them; then he saw a figure on a light pole in the center of the square. It was Karl, and he was waving wildly at Dale and Charlie.

Dale poked Charlie and pointed. "I hope he doesn't fall off."

General Packston then introduced Dale's grandfather and explained that he was a decorated military man himself who taught Dale the bugle calls that saved the town. Grandpa stood up proudly and waved to the crowd.

Next, the General introduced Dale's mother as one of the best Women's Air Service Pilots and someone all young women should look up to. Mother shyly stood up and waved to the crowd.

General Packston introduced Mr. Greenleaf and the crowd clapped enthusiastically as the general stepped back and the factory owner walked over to the podium carrying a black case.

Mr. Greenleaf set the case down and held his hand up for quiet. He began, "Two nights ago, two young boys did a most amazing thing. They rode through the town on their bikes, one playing a bugle and the other telling the volunteer firemen where the fire was. They saved my factory as well as the planes from the Air Force base. I'm here today to present Dale with one of the finest cornets ever made by our company, a gold-plated Connqueror model 48A cornet."

Mr. Greenleaf reached down and opened the case. He brought out a bright gold horn with ornate engraving on the bell and pearl valve buttons. "My company only has made a few gold-plated cornets that we sell to the finest soloists in the world, like Herbert L. Clark and Jules Levy. After learning of Dale's actions, I am here to present Dale with this special cornet." Charlie nudged Dale to get up as the crowd roared with delight. Dale stood but could barely take a step. The gold finish sparkled in the sunlight as Mr. Greenleaf walked over and put the cornet in Dale's hand. "Son, you are a credit to bugle players and musicians everywhere." Dale gently took the cornet and touched the beautiful engraving on the bell.

Then Mr. Greenleaf turned back to the audience and said, "Charlie Walsh, will you join Dale." Charlie jumped up, half of his shirt hanging out of his pants, and ran up to the podium. Mr. Greenleaf took an envelope out of his suit pocket and waved it in the air.

"I would like to make a donation of musical instruments to the school so that all of the students at Emerson School can start band this year."

The crowd roared, and Charlie began jumping up and down, shouting, "Finally, I can play trombone like Tommy Dorsey."

"We're on stage," Dale said as he grabbed him by the arm and pulled him back to their seats.

Mr. Greenleaf held up his hand again, signaling the crowd to be quiet. "I would now like to introduce Mr. Joe Maddy from Interlochen, Michigan. Back in 1928, I donated money to start a National Music Camp in the lake country of Northern Michigan, and Joe Maddy has been running it ever since."

Mr. Maddy, who had thick brown wavy hair, joined Mr. Greanleaf at the podium. "At the National Music Camp, we believe in developing the finest young musicians not only in the United States but also in the world," Mr. Maddy began.

He turned back to Dale, "Your talent is evident from what you did to save the factory." Then he smiled at Charlie and added, "And from seeing your excitement about playing like Tommy Dorsey a few minutes ago, there is no question in my mind that you also have a desire to succeed as a musician."

The crowd laughed and clapped loudly. Charlie looked down at the floor as he realized that Mr. Maddy was referring to his earlier outburst.

Mr. Maddy continued, "I would like to present scholarships to both of you to attend Interlochen after you have played for a few years. I commend you for all you have done for the town and look forward to seeing you at camp." And with that, he shook the boys' hands and presented each of them with an envelope.

General Packston returned to the podium. He turned to the boys and winked slyly, "Charlie, I hear…" and he leaned into the microphone as if to confide in the audience, "that you didn't even take time to change out of your pajamas when you rode through the town. Should I call you PJ instead of Charlie?"

Charlie blushed and whispered to Dale, "You promised not to tell!"

The crowd began to chant, "PJ, PJ," causing Charlie to grin widely and raise his hand in acknowledgment. After all, he was a hero, regardless of what he had been wearing at the time.

"Finally, as the commanding general at the Air Force base, I would like to present each of these boys with a First Cavalry pin to match the one Dale's grandfather gave him and an official Ranger patch in honor of Dale's father.

General Packston gave the boys each a pin and a patch and shook their hands.

"Would you like to say something?" General Packston asked the boys.

Sweat started running down Charlie's face as he approached the microphone. The crowd began to chant, "PJ—PJ—PJ—PJ"

"Thanks, everybody, we just wanted to help my dad and all the firemen. And also thanks for the swell pin and patch, General." The General nodded his head in approval and patted Charlie on the back.

Dale swallowed as he stepped next to Charlie and leaned into the microphone. "I don't know what to say, Mr. Greenleaf. This cornet is so beautiful," Dale said as he fingered the inlaid pearl tops of the valves. "I can't wait to start band with Mr. Jeffrey and all my friends."

Karl, who had been hanging on the light pole during all the speeches, whistled loudly, and Dale could hear the other kids in his class yelling his name. "I also want to thank Mr. Maddy for the scholarships to Interlochen. When I learn to play this," and Dale held up the shiny cornet for all to see, "I'm going to go to your camp. I also hope I can fish while I'm there."

Mr. Maddy leaned in behind Dale and said into the microphone, "That's what I like—a musician who also fishes. I'll have the boat and bait ready when you come," he laughed.

"Most of all," Dale continued and he turned to point at his grandfather, "I want to thank Grandpa for teaching me how to play the bugle."

Dale walked over to his chair behind the podium, placed the cornet back in its case and took the worn bugle from the leather case and returned to the podium. "The only way to honor another bugle player is with a bugle call. This is for you, Grandpa." Dale raised the bugle to his lips and played *First Cavalry*.

The notes were clear and solid, and the last one echoed around the buildings of the town square. Grandpa dabbed his eyes before giving Dale a big hug. The crowd once again clapped and cheered in approval.

General Packston ended the ceremony by inviting everyone for ice cream and a band concert by Mr. Goldman and his band.

The boys and their families went down the steps of the bandstand and the audience parted to let them pass. The townspeople crowded in to shake their hands or pat them on the back as the boys made their way to the table filled with cups of ice cream. Tommy and Victor pushed their way to the front. "I can't believe we can start an instrument!" Victor shouted in Dale's ear, and he shoved forward to grab a cup of ice cream.

Bridget and Chrissy surrounded Dale. "We're so proud of you!" and the girls kissed him at the same time on both cheeks.

Dale blushed as Tommy said, "AHHHHHHH!"

Charlie, who had been eyeing the ice cream, interrupted, "We'd better get moving before everyone eats all the ice cream."

Dale and his friends spent the rest of the afternoon eating ice cream and listening to the band concert. When the concert ended, the boys decided to walk home.

Just as they were leaving the square, two Jeeps full of soldiers roared up next to them.

Lieutenant Buck Jones hopped out of the first vehicle. "Not so fast, boys, we have one more gift from General Packston," and he gestured for the boys to jump into the Jeeps.

Victor excitedly shouted, "We get to ride in Jeeps with army guys?"

One of the soldiers in the back corrected him, "Not army guys—Airborne, son, Airborne."

The boys jumped in and were soon bouncing down the street with the wind blowing in their faces. When the Jeeps stopped they were at the Jungle by the start of the trail that led to the fort and where they had first met the soldiers.

"Follow us, boys," Lieutenant Jones ordered and the boys climbed out of the Jeeps and made their way down the trail behind the soldiers.

When they were halfway there, Lieutenant Jones stepped aside and said to Dale, "You lead the way now, and we'll follow." As the boys rounded the corner expecting to see their fort crushed by the big oak tree, they couldn't believe the their eyes. The tree was gone and the fort had new walls and a roof with a camouflage net over the top. In the front of the fort stood a flag pole with a black flag bearing the Airborne symbol flying proudly in the wind.

Charlie was breathing hard, both from the long walk down the trail and the excitement of the new fort. Karl peeked in one of the windows and motioned for Dale and the others to join him. Cautiously, Dale opened the door. Inside, hanging on the wall, was a green army helmet and a pair of binoculars for each of the boys. They put on the helmets and ran back outside.

Lieutenant Jones explained, "We rebuilt the fort while you were at the band concert as ordered by General Packston. The general had a fort when he was a boy, and since you saved his military base, he wanted to save your fort."

Charlie was so excited he hugged Lieutenant Jones. The soldier chuckled and announced that they had better get the boys home.

Dale was the last one to be dropped off. As the Jeep reached the top of Simpson Hill, Dale could see his family and Scout sitting on the porch. Dale began waving at them as the Jeep raced toward the house, his hair blowing in the wind.

When the Jeep screeched to a stop in front of the house, the lieutenant turned to Dale and said, "Sir, it has been my pleasure to serve you today," and he gave Dale a crisp salute.

Dale saluted back and jumped out. "Thanks for everything," he called as he ran up the stairs of the porch.

Grandpa stood up and asked, "Where've you been?"

"Let me tell you all about it at dinner," Dale said as he opened the front door. "I'm starved."

Dale's mom followed him inside. "This has been a very exciting day for everyone."

Dale sat down at the kitchen table. "It's just like Grandpa said, 'You have to enjoy every day of your life,'" he added as he shoveled the serving spoon into the bowl of mashed potatoes.

He looked at Grandma, "Do you think Grandpa and I can get out of doing the dishes tonight so I can practice my new cornet?"

Grandma frowned. "Here we go again with you and your grandfather getting out of doing the dishes...but yes, today, you have earned it." Grandpa winked at Dale, and asked for seconds of Grandma's meatloaf.

The End

ABOUT THE AUTHORS ...

Paul Kimpton grew up in a musical family and was a band director in Illinois for 34 years. His father Dale was a band director and professor at the University of Illinois, and his mother Barbara was a vocalist. When Paul is not writing, he is reading or enjoying the outdoors.

Ann Kimpton played French horn through college and went on to be a mother, teacher, and high school administrator. Her parents, Henry and Maryalyce Kaczkowski, both educators, instilled an appreciation for the fine arts and the outdoors in all of their children.

Ann and Paul were high school sweethearts who met when they played in the high school band. They have two grown children, Inga and Aaron, who share their love of music, the outdoors, and adventure. They now have a new grandson, Henry, who will continue the tradition.

Look for more books
in the *Adventures with Music* series

www.adventureswithmusic.net

#2: Dog Tags

The instruments arrive and the students have their first band rehearsal, but Dale has his mind on other things . . .

Grandpa knelt down and looked directly into Dale's eyes. "This is a very brave thing you're doing for your country, son. You're making the biggest sacrifice any boy can make by volunteering your dog for the military."

Breaking free from his grandfather, Dale ran to Scout and gave him one last deep hug. He whispered, "Do your best, Scout. I love you."